Sitting Opposite My Brother

SITTING OPPOSITE MY BROTHER

David Bergen

Turnstone Press

Turnstone Press
607 - 100 Arthur Street
Winnipeg, Manitoba
Canada R3B 1H3

Turnstone Press gratefully acknowledges the assistance
of the Canada Council and the Manitoba Arts Council.

"Where You're From," "The Fall," "The Bottom of the Glass,"
and "La Rue Prevette" first appeared in *Prairie Fire*.
These stories were also included in *The Journey Prize
Anthology*, Volumes 1, 3, 4 and 5.

Cover illustration: Steve Gouthro

Text design: Manuela Dias

This book was printed and bound in Canada by
Hignell Printing for Turnstone Press.

Canadian Cataloguing in Publication Data
Bergen, David, 1957 –
Sitting opposite my brother
ISBN 0-88801-172-5
I. Title.
PS8553.E74S58   1993   C813'.54   C93-098058-1
PR9199.3.B47S58   1993

for Mary

TABLE OF CONTENTS

THE BOTTOM OF THE GLASS

I DO NOT SUFFER WELL, AND THIS, IN THE FINAL totalling of my life, may be my greatest failure. To suffer well, I have been taught, is to find joy in pain, to be steadfast and fly beyond the temporal, to bear one's cross. Suffering well, it seems, describes the young Anabaptist man who, in 1528 at Bruck, on the Mur, and about to be drowned for his faith by the papistic Roman church, laughed at the water. Of course, some held that the devil had hardened his heart.

Lately I have caught myself gritting my teeth at the strangest of times. For instance, when I am relaxing: I will be sleeping or reading and suddenly become conscious of my mouth: I am clenching my teeth as if lifting something heavy or bracing myself for a fall. Aware of this, I force myself to relax; I drop open my mouth, yawn, breathe past my teeth, think of soothing images, but all I seem to get are balloons popping, the ocean pounding into me, and water drip, drip, dripping onto my forehead. So, I clench my teeth again.

Vange, my wife, says I should take drugs. Indocid, she says, because this is what she uses for her period cramps. She

1

says this to me across the supper table as I am feeding Leslie, who is spitting everything back at me.

"Take two," Vange says, "it'll knock you out."

"I don't want to be knocked out," I say. My jaw hurts. Our son Daniel used to grind his teeth at night; asleep, he'd suddenly be working away so hard you could hear him through the walls. When I was young my uncle told me a person's teeth never rot after they die, that death preserves teeth, that you could exhume the body a hundred years later and you'd still see the teeth, the mouth full of molars. He grinned at me as he said that, clicking and showing his fat purple tongue. The other day I thought of my uncle as I put my ear to the freshly dug black earth and listened for my son's teeth grinding up at me. Because he died this summer, my son did, just after his fifth birthday.

Ted Schmidt next door is an alcoholic. So is his wife and so was, perhaps, the wife before that. Personally, I used to like to drink with Ted because he was generous and good-natured, a man happy to have someone beside him nursing Johnnie Walker. We would sit on the front porch in the late afternoon and watch the setting sun through our drinks as we tipped our glasses, and Ted would say, *What a beautiful earth*, and I would nod in agreement. Ruthie, his wife, sometimes joined us and she would settle beside me, stretch her long legs down the stairs and bang ice against her teeth. We would talk about baseball or Marxism – Ruthie liked to talk about Marxism; she said once she'd like to be a good Marxist Christian. I wasn't sure why she said *good*. Anyways, I haven't had a drink with Ted and Ruthie since Danny died, which is just over two months now. I don't mean to harp on this, but it's at the core of what I'm saying. You see, he drowned in Ted and Ruthie's swimming pool. I suppose he thought he could swim. I imagine he thought, *Hey, neat, water, I'll swim.* I'm not sure what I suppose or think or imagine any more except I do know this is the reason I no longer drink with Ted. Also, two weeks after Daniel's funeral, Ted became a

Christian. He came over and showed me the Four Spiritual Laws and I said, "I know, Ted, I've seen those before." He said he wasn't drinking any more, that he was planning on going to church only he hadn't decided which one. It shouldn't be hard, I thought, our town of ten thousand has twenty-six churches. I said, "Good for you, Ted," as if he were sixteen and had just passed his driver's test. And then I asked, "How about Ruthie?"

And he smiled a dry, thirsty smile and said, "No, Ruthie is still Ruthie."

One of these days Vange is going to fly apart. She's been too calm, too reasonable, as if she is trying to tell me this too is life, that grief can turn you inside out so you don't let it, you turn your back on it, or you spit it out like bad fruit. I sat on the toilet tonight and watched her bathe Leslie. Leslie lay back on a frame of cloth and metal, and she gurgled and pushed plastic ducks into her mouth and she punched at the lights above our mirror. I could smell Zincofax and baby powder, and I looked at Vange's back, her spinal cord speed-bumping through her T-shirt, and thought how easy it was to make children. Vange wanted to last night. She said, "Now," and though we met and came apart, I felt I was deceiving Daniel, as if he could be so easily replaced. "It's good, this," Vange whispered into my throat, "this is what we need," and I shuddered because she sounded desperate and her face was wet, and I was unable to say *Yes* or *No*, so I thought of Ruthie, next door, drinking alone while her husband poured through the Bible. I have nothing against the Bible. I know the stories by heart. I told them to Daniel as he squeezed his hot little body in beside me on our green armchair. David fucked Bathsheba, Lot's daughters fucked Lot, Herod butchered babies, Salome demanded John the Baptist's head on a dish. Great. But really, no, for Daniel I kept things simple: I erased the messages of sin and salvation from the stories that had once converted me at a young age. And, after all that effort, one night he lifted his face and

3

breathed on me, his head still damp from his bath, and he asked why Grandpa said that Jesus died for all the little Daniels of the world.

Grandpas. My father, who lives in this same town, is retired now. A pious man, my father suffers well. He would gladly have been a sixteenth-century martyr. For him the kingdom of God is in heaven, not on earth, and to have been drowned in a sack or burned alive would have given him great joy. Sometimes when I visit him at his home he watches my face and I see he is ashamed of me; he sees his own image and he recoils. So I think maybe I should hit him or walk away but I don't. I stay longer and make him suffer. It was at Daniel's funeral, watching my father grieve, that I realized there was not much difference between the bottom of my glass and his heaven.

To keep busy, he reads the Bible and *Martyr's Mirror*. I walk into his musty house, sit beside him, and stare at his white hair, and at his trembling fingers holding his books, one of which is opened to stories of martyrs: Richst Heynes, 1547, "thrust into a bag like an irrational brute, and cast into the water and drowned"; Claes Lecks, 1548, burned alive; Elizabeth, 1549, "to be drowned in a bag – and thus offered up her body to God"; six brethren at Amsterdam, on the 20th of March 1549, "ended their lives in great joy, and were burned alive." I have read these stories and think I under-stand why my father is so disappointed in me; he sees Daniel's death as useless (as do I), but he also blames me for his death because I have failed to carry the seed, to pass on the essence of life. *Fate* and *chance* are words my father does not use. For my father a martyr's death is the ideal death be-cause it disguises the finality of things – of course, he would not admit to this. It produces a credible story, a name and a date to be remembered. A sort of posterity. A martyr's death, as I see it, is an unreal death filled with impossible expecta-tion, idealism and stupidity. Of course we all want to be remembered. But we won't be.

Funny. Vange is going to church with Ted. From the kitchen window I watch them disappear around the corner of Oak and Henry; Ted with his short red hair, his orange neck, and Vange, her hair long and blonde, her skirt swaying at her calves. Vange is still breast-feeding so she takes Leslie in the big red Gendron. This Sunday, after they are out of sight, I wander around the house and then I lie on Daniel's bed. We've cleaned out his room for guests but I can still smell him. Then, as these August nights can bring frost, I go out to check the garden. I'm crouching over the cherry tomatoes when suddenly Ruthie is there. She's wearing shorts so I'm staring at her bare legs and when I look up, following her smooth thighs past her crotch to her stomach and neck, I see she is dressed warmer on top, a grey kangaroo sweatshirt. She's wearing red lipstick, smiling or perhaps pouting, and she's holding a drink, either vodka or water. I know which it is.

"Ted's gone," she says.

I stand and nod, stretch my back, and Ruthie's hair is wet and smells good and I am aware of liking the look and smell of a woman just out of the bath.

She asks, "Wanna drink?"

I hesitate, look down at my tomatoes, see her toes which are painted purple, and I say, *Okay.* So we go to her house, where I sit on a stool at the kitchen counter and watch her long fingers crack ice out of a tray and drop it into a glass. From where I sit I see the pool and it's really quite nice, in the shape of a light-bulb with the shallow end the screw-in part, and I force myself to look at it, study its length and imagine its depth. Ruthie sits across the counter from me, sees where I'm looking, and says, *Sorry.* She stands to draw the curtain, but I tell her that it's fine, that it's just a goddamn pool, so she shrugs and says that Ted wants to fill it in, make it into a tennis court. They've put locks on all the gates now, she says, and then she says more but I'm concentrating on my drink, which feels like it's the first of a few for the day.

5

Ruthie stops talking. I say, "Ted seems happy these days."

Ruthie says, *Yaa*, and then says she's hot so she takes off her kangaroo top. She's wearing a pink tank top underneath, and when she swivels on her stool and reaches for the bottle, I see the white of her breast and her nipple. Her nipple is small and her breast is tight and firm. She's never had children. Normally, I would glance away but today I don't. Perhaps I feel she owes me something and if this is it I'll take it because obviously she's aware of her own body and what it does. She swings back at me and while she pours another drink I study her. She has a small stingy mouth. Her neck is long and her body is still fine but it's her face and eyes, her hands too, that tell me who she is. She lights a cigarette, offers me one and I take it. She smiles and touches my hand which is lying on the counter. She says, "Ted's on the edge. To be honest, he was happier before. This Christianity is wearing him out." Ruthie doesn't sound happy or cynical. She is matter-of-fact, and I wonder if she wants Ted to start drinking again. I imagine *Yes* and *No*, always yes and no. Personally, I admire Ted. He's not hiding anything, never has, and that goes against the rules in our town. On the surface, our town is a perfect little place – excellent lawns, no slums (perhaps because there is no railroad track), houses freshly painted – it fairly gleams. But beneath the surface it's an ocean teeming with its own life; a life of desires and rot and failures that, in any other place, would be quite accepted (or if not accepted, accommodated), but here people either ignore the life below the surface or they coldly chase the culprits out, all the while saving the appearances – except they have never really gotten to Ted Schmidt, and I have to admire him.

Ruthie begins to talk about the second Donut Shop she and Ted are starting, about hiring young girls and buying new equipment, and while her little mouth grimaces I wonder why I'm sitting in her house on a Sunday morning drinking and looking down her pink tank top. I mean, if I want to look at breasts I just have to ask Vange, she's good to me. "I have to go," I say. "I promised Vange I'd pick her up from church and then we're going out to eat."

"Oh," she says, sorry, it seems, to see me leave. "I guess Ted'll walk home on his own."

"I guess," I say, becoming aware at the door of Ruthie's smell of liquor, smoke and shampoo, and how tall she is and how her eyes slant down to her nose and the sheen of her legs and how all I'd have to do is pull her near whichever way I wanted and push my knee up between her because she is feeling it too, her eyes travelling my face, my legs, but it's her mouth that decides for me. So I touch her cheek, rosy, rosy, and tell her not to worry about Ted, which is silly because she's not.

We go to eat at the hotel. Ordinarily, we'd stop at McDonald's but Leslie doesn't care where we eat. Vange is wearing a white skirt and a loose yellow top. She has on white sandals and her tanned feet glow under the dash. I touch her leg as I drive and she takes my hand. The Gendron is stashed in the trunk where it bumps and clangs round the corners. Leslie nods off in the car seat in the back.

"Lots of stares today," Vange says.

"Well, what did you expect?" I say, and then, "How about Ted?"

"Ted has moved beyond guilt and shame, and his conversion is, in their eyes, the fruit of all this. And maybe that's the way we should see it too. People get pleasure in seeing Ted and me in church together, even though I can smell their desire to ask after you."

I ask, "Why is it that believers can't see irony? Is life that simple for them?"

Vange isn't paying attention. She says, "One woman, Mrs. Wiebe, well-intentioned I'm sure, pulled me aside and whispered that she was sorry, so sorry, and asked how we were, and before I could say we were fine, she was explaining that there were two ways we could deal with this: I could be angry and bitter or I could see this as an opportunity, like Ted Schmidt, she said. Like Ted. She actually said that."

"Which Wiebe?" I ask.

"I don't know, don't care." Vange sighs and trails my knuckles with her nails. We pull into the hotel parking lot.

"What?" I say. "That I should stop drinking too?" Then, not waiting for an answer, I say, "I saw Ruthie."

Vange looks surprised. "Oh, where?"

"Outside. In our garden."

"She actually came outside?"

"Yes, and then I went to her house for a drink."

Vange doesn't say anything. She kneels on the front seat and reaches back to unstrap Leslie. She cradles her and climbs out. Vange doesn't like Ruthie. She thinks Ruthie is unsafe. In fact, once she said that Ruthie was too sexy, as if warning me, and she said too that Ruthie cared only about Ruthie and that made her dangerous.

Actually, I do see what she means but I find Ruthie more pathetic than dangerous – like Ted, or maybe like me, I think. After we're seated and we've ordered, I ask Vange if she thinks she's grieved enough. She drinks some water, looks at me and says, "Yes." When she says this she looks just like Daniel used to when he tried to convince me of something: *not a lie, Dad.* Then she says grieving is like climbing a mountain, you reach a certain level and then you descend; she says she has peaked and she will never grieve enough, but that she has gone high enough.

I believe her, because for her life has two laws, natural and human, and Danny's death falls under natural. I wonder if she considers habitual and driven drinking a natural law too, because for me I still hold Ted and Ruthie responsible. I mean, how does a sodden son-of-a-bitch like Ted apply mouth-to-mouth? Through a bottle? Right now, sitting across from Vange, I am angry at her fatalism. I remember a night several weeks after Danny died. Vange was looking for something to take hold of, and she was going on about these natural laws and I harumphed and said, "Solomon Grundy, born on Monday, christened on Tuesday, married on Wednesday, took ill on Thursday, worse on Friday, died on Saturday, buried on Sunday. This is the end of Solomon Grundy." I paused and then said, "I'd say that was a full life, wouldn't you?"

"Don't do this to me," Vange said. "You can't leave me out of this. I'll end up hating you."

I backed off then, scared suddenly, and even now if I am angry at her I will not walk that edge of her. I reach across the table and hold the sleeve of her yellow top between my thumb and forefinger. Vange looks at me. I can feel her soft skin on the back of my finger, and she smiles, a kind of grieving smile.

The bottom of the glass is a bit of a paradox. In the right light, with the right drink and right glass, the bottom can bend and twist just perfect, so that you want to put your tongue down there and stroke it, or maybe drink quickly in order to reach the bottom, but then the beauty of it disappears with the liquor. So you get more, there's always more, and you sniff it, inhaling the fumes, but the bottom is still swimming there so pretty and it'd be good to see it again. Only this time you maybe drop a marble in there for further effect, reach in two fingers, remove the fingers, savour them in your mouth, watch the marble spin round and round and you drink quickly, absurdly, trying to reach the bottom of the glass.

I attempt to explain all this to Vange but she has little patience for theories involving alcohol. She wonders how long I will go on using the glass as my way of mourning. And me, I don't know. I want to tell her that she, Vange, has always been my salvation, but that would be admitting that these days she's not enough.

Ed, one of the reporters at the paper where I work, says I should take a holiday. He watches my hands shake at ten o'clock in the morning and he says I should do something.

He says *take a holiday* but he means something else. I shrug and laugh nervously but still go for lunch and have a few drinks and before getting back to work I reach under my car seat and take a few pulls of Scotch. So, for the afternoon I'm fine, and when I get home I fix a drink and moon over it before settling into the kitchen and helping Vange with supper. I tell her Ed says we should take a holiday. She says, "Fine," and suddenly we're planning two weeks at the lake, which frightens me because it's too close to water and too far away from the secrecy of the bottle.

"It'll be good for us. My mom and dad said we could use their cabin any time," Vange says, wedging tomatoes, the light glancing off the burnished knife.

I get two weeks. Vange works as an accountant out of the house, so there's no problem there, and Leslie's all gung-ho for the cabin and mosquitoes and fires in the evening. I can see the excitement in her blue eyes as I bend to rub noses with her: "Heeeeah, Lessey, betchabetchabetcha." She throws her head back, grabs a fistful of my cheek and says, "Bung." I go over to ask Ted and Ruthie to watch the house and water the lawn. Ruthie answers the door. She's eating doughnuts, and icing sugar lies like dandruff on the shoulders of her black top. Then Ted is there too, hovering behind Ruthie, one hand on her backside, and when I say what we're doing Ruthie says, "Sure, no problem," but Ted looks surprised, as if we're deserting him. I'm not sure why he feels that way. "Wanna come in?" Ruthie asks, but I say, "No, gotta pack."

In the early mornings when light begins to filter through the tops of the trees and touch the bedroom curtains, Leslie and I leave Vange sleeping in the cabin and we walk down to the boardwalk that leads to the big campground at Falcon Lake. As I bump the stroller slowly over the rotting wood, Leslie giggles, claps her hands, and oohs at the rushes and birds, the muskrats, and at her own ability to ooh. We tread the dewy grass at the edge of the beach, listen to the tock of axes beating on wood and smell bacon. Here at the lake I find I can manage without the fumes rising constantly from the glass to my nostrils. The back of my throat doesn't ache, either. Sure, the edge is always there, especially in the late afternoon, after a swim and while contemplating dinner. But I can handle it. Vange says it's Ruthie, we live too close to her and Ted, and maybe we should move. Yes, she says again, we should move, and she smiles at the thought. When she says things like this I wonder how much longer she will put up with me; although here, away from there, we are warming to each other again.

On the beach in the afternoons Vange and I lie side by side and touch hands as we watch Leslie burrow in the sand. Then Vange swims. She walks self-consciously to the edge of the lake. I watch her move, study her shoulder-blades, the roll of her bum. Sometimes I whistle. Once she is in the water she smiles back from her bodiless head. She bobs, she dunks, she seals, she disappears. I hold my breath and smell my arms, which give off a mixture of lotion and sweat. I stoop and smell Leslie and she is a bun freshly drawn from the oven. Vange surfaces out past the buoys and I breathe easier when I see her head ploughing along. She was the one teaching Daniel to swim. He'd just come off the water wings and this summer was going to learn the crawl. Vange turns on her back. Leslie piles sand on my thighs. This one time a young girl, maybe eighteen, runs by. She's wearing a black bikini and her stomach is flat and tanned and her teeth are white. She is beautifully awkward; coltish. Two boys, her age, follow, young and foolish and hopeful. I pat Leslie's head and ask if she's hot. "Gig," she says, so I help her dig.

Eating supper on our last evening before heading back home, Vange looks up at me and says, "It's exactly three months."

"Yes," I say, "I know," and I wonder if there comes a time when one stops counting, when the sight of a shoe lying mateless at the door is simply that, a shoe. I would like a drink. Not the cold beer sitting before me, but something whitish or yellowish in a heavy glass, something that brings with it a shuddered warmth, a deep familiar sadness. But there is nothing in the cabin. I consider the possibilities of driving into Falcon to purchase some peace, but it is raining hard tonight and Vange hates to be left alone with Leslie. Vange is watching me; she senses my thoughts but says nothing.

While she puts Leslie down I build a fire and open a book. I close the book. I check the shutters for leaks. I sit down and poke at the fire. I put on my jacket and go outside and start the car. Lightning screams in off the lake. Thunder rolls up our dock. The lights go out in the cabin and come back on again. I turn the car off and go back inside. I shake my jacket off at the door, and drops of water float back into my face. Vange is at the fire, stirring it like a cauldron, and I see her shoulders are shaking. I push my wet hair behind my ears with icy fingers. She is wearing an old grey sweater of her father's and it has a big collar that comes up to Vange's crown, and from where I sit it makes her head look small, her back crooked. Finally, she turns and her face is ugly and raw and she calls my name, *Saul,* and this makes me move. It takes me a long time but I reach her and hold her and I say, "Good girl, that's a good girl."

"Good girl," I say.

We leave late in the afternoon the following day and our usual three-hour drive is extended because of blueberry picking, a flat tire and a hot front-seat bit of love beneath some bushes off the side of the highway while Leslie sleeps heavy and oblivious in the back seat. We stop for a late supper and creep into our driveway as the sky is turning dark. I turn off the ignition and feel the heaviness of everything come sliding back into me. Vange feels the same, I can see it. There's loud music thumping from Ted and Ruthie's, and lots of cars are parked in their driveway.

"Party," Vange says. She sounds disappointed, aware by now that this is Ted's party too, and immediately I want to apologize, to start the car, to leave this again and for good.

But instead I say, "I'll take Leslie." I carry Leslie up to bed and Vange tucks her in while I clean out the rest of the car. Then I go inside and lean on the kitchen sink and look out over the yard to Ted and Ruthie's where fully clothed grown-ups are jumping into the pool. I am sure I see Ted, gangly and hoarse-voiced, patrolling the pool, his arm around whoever comes near, and it must be this image of his brazen manner, his disregard for holding to the faith, any faith, that makes me angry, and suddenly I am crossing the lawn and knocking at his front door.

I ring and knock and ring, for some reason refusing to open it myself, and finally Ted answers, big smile on his red face, hands full of glasses, and he pulls up, squints and says, "Aww, fuck, you know, aww shit, Saul." And then, with cunning, he pushes a glass at me, "Wanna?" and for some reason I take one and hold it close. It's bourbon, I'm sure, and though I want to weep with gratitude, I don't touch it. I just look at it. Ted checks behind me: "Vange?" I shake my head. He seems relieved. In the living-room I see Ruthie slow-dancing with Al Krahn; they're holding each other up, Al with his hand running her back. The door behind me is still open, and if I turn and walk straight I will reach my own house. Ted isn't asking me in, nor is he chasing me out. He shifts from foot to foot and mutters *fuck* once in a while, for my benefit, I guess, but he's not as drunk as he's pretending. His eyes, when they hold mine, are dark clear holes in which I see all that is important, and I understand that right now he hates me, hates Ruthie and Al Krahn behind him, hates the glasses he holds, the glass I hold, and, most important, he wants me to drink from mine.

Without warning I say, "Tell me how you found him."

"How?"

I nod.

"The gate was unlocked," he says. "I came out for an early morning swim and he was there at the bottom of the pool. The shallow end."

This shocks me and it must be evident because Ted asks me if I want to sit. I say no. For some reason I had imagined him floating face down in the water, his blond hair floating like a halo around his head, his shoulders to the open air; that was important, that he have some contact with the air. Ted's revelation makes everything seem farther away; now I will have to restructure things in my head, start this futile process again. Ted is babbling, saying something about how heavy he was, mouth-to-mouth, so much water, Ruthie biting her own knuckles till they bled, how this has driven a wedge into his marriage, but I only hear the words, the meaning is unimportant now. Over Ted's shoulder I watch Ruthie kiss Al and I can smell corn chips, can smell my bourbon. I am looking through a viscous liquid or perhaps an imperfect glass while Vange is whispering salvation in my ear from across the lawn, from Leslie's room. Ted suddenly screams at no one, "Shut the fucking music down." This brings me around and I look up expectantly, as if searching for someone. I realize I'm still holding my glass and that the liquor is untouched. Maybe it should stay that way, but then the glass will stay full and I can see at the bottom way down there an angel, its image warping up at me, and I need to rescue that angel, even though it's a hundred miles away.

THE VOTE

BEFORE THE VOTE WE TALKED ABOUT HIM. AND ABOUT his wife. Myrna Peters said that as a couple they were strong. Jake was a natural leader and Grace was a real helpmate. "You can see it by the way they talk to each other. They'll be a real model for our younger couples," she concluded. Her nostrils flared. They always did that when she believed strongly in something. She sometimes sang on Sunday mornings and her nostrils flared then too. Thomas, her husband, sat beside her and nodded agreement. He was a slow-moving grain farmer who claimed that Myrna was the best cook in the church. He was probably right.

Peter Fast stood up, cleared his throat and said that as far as he was concerned the problem didn't lie with Jake, who was a good man, but with Grace, who wore a different dress every Sunday and too many necklaces and was that befitting a servant of God, he asked.

"Here, here," cried George Neufeld, and even he seemed a little surprised by his short barks. But that didn't stop him from saying that there were some days when Grace looked like a woman of the streets she wore so much make-up, and he didn't think his own daughter Jenny should have a pastor's wife like that for a role model. We were all quiet for a bit after that until Frank Klassen, one of the lay preachers, asked, "But can he preach?" and we all agreed that he could.

Flora Penner got up then and passed Styrofoam cups around and poured coffee and we ate rhubarb platz that Grace had sent (Jake and Grace were at home waiting for the outcome of the vote) and we chewed quietly. Then Tim Martin said that Jake and Grace were probably no different from any of us and in the end it didn't really matter how many bracelets Grace wore on her wrists, or if she painted her fingernails pink or lavender, but it did matter if she loved the Lord and he thought that yes she did love the Lord and in the end he would vote for Jake.

June Kehler was pulling apart her Styrofoam cup and chewing on it and spitting little pieces onto the table. Her blonde hair was permed and cut short, and she finally said that she did have some trouble with Jake and Grace having air-conditioning in their house and she asked if their lifestyle was compatible with church-work and would they be able to cut back on their excessive lifestyle. Someone else added that Grace had been spoiled as a child; her father had not only spared the rod but had given her lots of *things*. Basically, she was selfish.

"Quite right," Bob, June's husband, said. "She wants a lot and it seems Jake has a hard time saying no. He'll be making, what? twenty-eight thousand a year plus expenses and I don't think any of us would complain about that but it sure won't buy Grace a new dress every week." George Neufeld jumped back into the fray and questioned Jake's theological base. Wasn't it maybe too liberal, he asked. He said that he didn't want his daughter Jenny being pummelled with words like *myth* and *evolution*.

"No one ever said Jake was against the creation story," Frank Klassen said. "He simply questioned whether God couldn't work through something like the Big Bang."

George shook his black hair. "It's all too haphazard," he said. "It would be like us putting a pen into a hat with a bunch of papers, shaking it up and coming up with the Bible. Uh, uh." He shook his head again, thinking, we were sure, of his poor Jenny.

Tim Martin's face was red. "I don't think whether or not Jake and Grace drive a new Honda or have certain *things* or even use a particular kind of birth control or believe in the Big Bang will make any difference on their effectiveness here in our congregation." He stopped and glared. We were feeling a little uncomfortable with the picking apart of Jake and Grace, but there was another side of us that also wanted to stretch things out a little further, a part of us that wondered what kind of birth control Jake and Grace *were* using.

Myrna spit it out for us. "And why don't they have children yet? They've been married seven years. Is it fair to ask a childless couple to relate to and counsel families?"

Miss Dyck, one of the older people at the meeting, raised her head at that point and said firmly that she had never had children, either, and she could not understand why couples with children always thought they were more well-rounded than childless couples, or single people for that matter. Hadn't in fact Paul implied that those who married were the weaker ones – "Better to marry than to burn," she said, and added that maybe, just maybe, Jake and Grace couldn't have children, even if they wanted them anyway.

We all bit at our rhubarb platz. Flora Penner said, "Maybe it's the make-up, it halts fertility."

Frank Klassen, who was chairing the meeting, ignored Flora and addressed Miss Dyck. "I like what you said, Elaine. It brings a human side to a pastor couple when you think of them wanting children but not able to have them. I think that's real necessary."

Miss Dyck nodded and sipped at black coffee. She was glowing from the compliment. Frank continued: "Maybe we should focus all of this a little bit and concentrate on Jake as a person. In the Pros we'd be getting a good preacher, a good-looking man, a counsellor, a young vital talent, and in the Cons we'd have someone who likes golf too much, has a temper, no children, and dabbles in liberal thinking." We watched the list go up on the blackboard. The chalk squeaked and Frank rolled on his heels. He said, "It isn't exactly that we have many other choices at this point. Well, that's not really true. The vote is *yes* or *no*. Kind of like a communist country vote, isn't it?" He laughed. "Which is crumbling all around us. Anyway, if you think Jake and Grace should be our pastor couple you mark *yes*. If not, you write *no*. Any more discussion needed?" He paused and we watched him, fidgeted a bit, and then June Kehler began to cut up pieces of paper. The basement was getting hot, and Harold, the volunteer custodian, turned down the thermostat. Mrs. Kehler put one piece of paper in front of each of us and we all wrote something, folded the paper and gave it back to Frank and June, who counted the votes. They conferred for a minute and then Frank said that Jake and Grace would be our next pastor couple. We decided that Tim would telephone immediately, before we began discussion on the new bathroom, and tell Jake and Grace the good news.

HOPE

IT BEING A HOT AFTERNOON, MY FATHER AND I TOOK refuge in an air-conditioned building that turned out to be a second-hand clothes store run by a man wearing a cone-shaped hat. My father, spurred by the possibility of a bargain, chose two shirts, one plaid, the other tan with pearled buttons, and began to barter. But he ran up against a wall; the owner refused to bend. The price on the tag was firm, he said. And when my father, typically, persisted, pointing out a frayed cuff and a badly mended collar, the man broke into Turkish and chased us from the store. Outside, I stood by myself in the shade of an awning. My father, by the curb, turned to me and shrugged. He said, "You think I should go back in there and plough him, don't you?"

I shook my head. I wasn't thinking that at all and I could tell my father was leading up to a speech. He continued, "I'm bigger, he's fatter and slower, right? But why? I'd just hurt my hand. It'd swell up. Do me no good. No good at all. Gotta watch out for men like that, they want people to react. They're angry and they think everybody else is angry. Full of malice. That's what. Not me. Uh, uh." He turned and grinned at the sight of my mother pulling up to the curb in the station wagon, new tires all around. His big palm came up, he motioned to me, and danced towards the car and the expectant faces of his family.

My father liked to move; the rest of us followed. It made little sense, he claimed, to dig a hole like a fox or build a nest like a bird and wait to die. My mother said that he panicked at the thought of sitting still. She said this calmly, having long ago accepted, it seemed, her fate as a nomad.

This time we were moving to Hope, B.C. It was 1968. Two years earlier we had moved from Prince George to Saskatoon. Saskatoon was okay. And then my father convinced yet another school that he was the principal it needed. So, Hope. My father said it gratefully, "We are going to Hope," as if this were a lucky place and not just a dot on the map at which he had arbitrarily thrown the dart of his resumé.

I was in love with my mother. And though nothing ever came to fruition, this love filled the days of my thirteenth year. I was nudged by happy shame as I imagined my brother, sisters and father dying, and I diving into the open arms of my mother, burying myself in her honeyed breasts, being wrapped in her long freckled arms. All this had nothing to do with deception or greed, but with the simple fact that I was smitten. And, I will admit today, never since have I felt the wonderful panic of lost love, of time flying, of time slowed, of jealously guarded seconds spent smelling a woman beside me, of the sickness unto death upon seeing how happy a woman can be with a husband. She knew; she had to know. I took her careful flirtings, a lingering kiss on the lips, her coy smiles thrown backwards in passing, the way she let me see her in various stages of undress, to be proof of her love. I think I see now that she trod an edge, as mothers must do. She neither made the situation laughable, nor took it too seriously, as if she were saying, *Yes, this is a fey love, but I won't strangle it.*

With our new tires we hummed along, playing Twenty Questions – hot, cold – the windows wide open, the air, as if from a furnace, whipping our ears and cheeks. Then my father started on riddles. He called them *conundrums*. He'd say a little rhyme or give us a situation and from that we had to ask questions that required yes or no answers until we'd find the solution. The first few were easy, but then my father said he had a big one, a tough one, a grand prize kind of conundrum. His voice teased, "If he had seen the sawdust, he would not have died." This was so vague and senseless that my sister and brother dropped out, complaining of thirst and boredom. I persisted, getting nowhere. Finally my mother joined in, and her first question, "Was he a blind midget?" was so good my father accused her of knowing the riddle. "Do not," she said. Together my mother and I battered my father until we had all the facts but no answer. Both of us understood that the answer required a twist of logic, a novel approach, and though so far we had shared information, suddenly it seemed we were divided, hiding thoughts and ideas from each other. Then my mother pointed a finger in the air and said, "I have it." While she explained her answer, I watched her, wondering at how easily she brushed me aside in the flush of victory. But she was wrong. Not completely, of course, and it was her wrong answer that gave me the solution. I spoke slowly then, to my father, knowing my mother was observing me carefully, and when my father nodded and said, "Yes, that's it," she looked perplexed, as if I'd robbed her of something. But this passed and she said, "Oh, Kenny, wonderful, perfect," kissing me just below the ear, leaving a wet spot. My father was looking at me in the rear-view mirror, a tired smile on his face, as if thinking I was too cocky for my own good.

In the late afternoon we took a detour into Drumheller because my father said the hills there were beautiful in an ugly sort of way, and he thought dinosaurs used to live there;

maybe we'd see some bones. My mother glanced at her watch. "Where will we tent tonight, Arnie?"

"No problem."

"Right," my mother sighed.

My father pulled at an eyebrow. "One more time the reluctant king, eh Irene?"

Mother's face reddened. She understood this was what happened when my father was tired. He attacked her. He dredged up old arguments, like the abdicating king and his brother. For some reason my father disliked royalty, particularly King George VI, and he told my mother this so often it seemed she began to oppose him for the sake of balance. Now, she pounced back. With the wind snatching her words, she said, "Of course George wasn't brilliant but he was efficient. And better a reluctant ruler than a disgraced Edward, more interested in sport with a common foreigner. Who was divorced and Catholic, to boot. In fact, every country, or family, or whatever, needs its capable leader. And on that, Arnie, you must agree." My father laughed and pulled my mother's ear. Finally, she smiled back and held his hand.

Two hours later I was alone with my mother. I was leaning over her shoulder, smelling her hair, which made me think of the rain, watching the push of her chest against her dress as the baby cried for milk. My chin lay on the sticky vinyl seat, my nose touched her sharp shoulder, my cheek brushed her dusty hair, and while she cooed to the baby she unbuttoned her dress and laid the grasping mouth in close, and I smelled the milk and heard the rhythmic pull of the baby's feeding. She patted the little head and then reached up to pat my cheek. "Walk around a bit, dear," she said, squinting into the sunlight outside the car. But I didn't want to walk around. Instead, I closed my eyes and listened to my baby sister feed, felt the rise and fall of my mother's body, while in the background, out there away from us, came the sounds of my father talking, the mechanic grunting, my older sister Cora giggling, and my younger brother Amis shuffling his feet on the asphalt and throwing rocks across the highway.

When we'd rolled, engine silent, onto the Texaco lot, my father had pointed at the mechanic walking towards us and said, "Oh my, a hippie," and my mother had said, "So, fine, take your saviours as they come." Now I was watching my father through the crack in the raised hood. He pulled at his wallet, thinking about money, but then he suddenly dived back under the hood, aiding the man beside him. My mother pulled baby Allie off her breast. Her nipple was shiny and stretched. She leaned her head out the window and told Cora to get off the car. "Look at you," she said. "You're filthy" – and added 'dear' as an afterthought. "Will she never learn," my mother asked me, "that first there are boys and then there are men?" I didn't say anything. I was studying the soft fuzz at her nape. She unfolded herself and stood in the hot sun, tall and big-jawed, her face pink, one hand holding the baby, the other fumbling with the nubbed buttons of her dress. I watched her walk across the lot to the bathroom, and the late afternoon sun spilled through her dress so that I could see her body outlined, its shape undulating through the haze.

I climbed from the car and back into the world. I felt sinful, repentant, happy, and washed over with a little madness. Though not too mad. I was quite happy to live love as an echo, conjuring wonderful domestic scenes of my mother and I twinned in easy chairs by a fire, idly discussing the merits of Queen Elizabeth II and her charming boys, while my mother clicked knitting needles and spun a red sweater for me, her son.

My father was bartering. The radiator needed replacing and though the mechanic claimed differently, my father was sure a used one could be found. Finally, the mechanic flipped his pony-tail and said, "Good, then go find one." This stymied my father. He circled the car, he eyed the hills, but eventually gave in, only to sputter once again upon hearing that the car wouldn't be ready until morning, it being Saturday night.

My father hated long hair. He hated Pierre Trudeau. When Trudeau was elected prime minister, Father turned his back on the TV and left the room. He was not always intolerant – there were just certain things that made his face twist in frustration: long hair, the monarchy. The year before we moved to Hope, a draft-dodger came to our town. He was living with the United Church minister and one day, for some reason, was eating ice-cream at our kitchen table. He didn't say much, just ate copious amounts of ice-cream. My mother served and my father sat across from him and asked questions.

"What's the point?"

"Point?" the draft-dodger said.

"Why are you running?"

The fellow, who had long hair caught in a pony-tail, looked up with a perplexed smile, but he just asked for more ice-cream.

"I mean," my father said, "is there some reason for dodging the draft other than it being the thing these days? Like, do you have religious reasons?"

"Sure, I believe the human body is created by a greater power, and that includes me, my own body, and I don't like the idea of shrapnel piercing my flesh."

My father said he was a C.O. during World War II. "A conscientious objector," he expanded.

The draft-dodger licked his spoon and eyed my father with what seemed respect. "Really?"

"Yes, and the point wasn't my own flesh but the stupidity of war." My father tapped the table. "Bring everything down to a personal level, the example of my wife and me. I get angry, I don't hit her."

"Some men do."

"But I can't and there's the crux. If I do, I forfeit what I believe: hope; that violence destroys the doer; that an eye for an eye makes everyone blind. I like you and your kind. Except you don't know why you're doing this. And besides, you should get your hair cut. People might listen to you then."

"Ah," said the man, a light passing his long face, a smile on his lips. "But I would have fought against Hitler."

My father threw his hands at the ceiling. His Adam's apple bobbed. "You see what I mean?" he cried to my mother, to me. Me, standing in the doorway, wishing I had long hair like that draft-dodger.

We had enough money, my father said, to repair the car and take a hotel room for the night. The hotel turned out to be the motel across from the Texaco. We had two beds and a kitchenette. The baby lay sleeping on one of the beds and Amis kicked at the TV, which wouldn't work. My mother sat on a chair in the kitchenette and stared at the hot plate while my father showered. For some reason the room depressed her. Cora said she was going out to look around. My mother waved a hand at her, said she had a headache and took two Aspirin, tossing her head back to force the pills down her throat. Then she stood and put a kettle on, opened some cupboard doors, found some Nescafe and spooned a bit into a cup. Amis got a picture – a Bob Hope special – and he and I lay on the bed while the black and white flicker filled the room. My mother came over and laid a hand on Amis. She was sitting beside me, she was wearing a long T-shirt and panties, and I could feel the softness of her thigh on my arm. Her knees were rough and round and a little red.

"Those are The Beatles," she said, pointing at the TV. Then my father came out of the bathroom, a towel around his waist, and snorted, "The Beatles. A bug. Imagine."

I turned from the TV and looked at my father's hairy chest and big shoulders. He found some shorts and slipped them on under his towel. Then he removed the towel and snapped it at my mother, grinning. "Fun, Irene, eh? Nice little romantic place."

"Hmm." She didn't look at him. She kept her hand on Amis. She'd folded her legs so that one of her knees lay on my back. "We need some soup. Soup and bread. Butter too. Sandwich meat if you can, and pop. For the kids."

My father dressed and left, and my mother stood and slowly walked to the bathroom. She turned to look back and smiled weakly, picking up a towel from the stand by the door. She showered, taking a long time, and when the baby was getting restless Amis wanted to call her but I said, *No, let her be.* She came out of the shower, her face rosy from the steam, and she stood in the kitchenette raking her long hair. I watched the movement of her body as she stroked her head. My father returned with a bag of food. He opened a tin of soup and said, "Where's Cora?"

"Outside somewhere," my mother said. The baby woke up and my mother gave it her breast. She closed her eyes as the baby fed.

"Out there?" my father asked, pointing outside. "This is not my idea of a great place to have our daughter walking the streets."

"If I recall, you're the one who chose this great place."

"Why is it," my father asked, "that I am the only one who can control that girl's coming and going?" He was standing over the hot plate, stirring soup. He was angry. The back of his neck was moving. And then my mother said that *he* was so respected because *he* had made his children memorize Ephesians 6. After she said this, my father kept quiet, spooning soup into bowls.

We ate around a card-table, my father constantly looking at the door, my mother bouncing an unhappy baby, saying in a soothing voice, "Okay, there, shhh, shhh, it's okay." After the meal she sat on the bed with the baby at her side and ran an emery board over her heels.

When Cora came in everyone looked up, waiting. Cora was bright-eyed, her hair pushed back as if she'd sat in front of a fan, her cheeks glowing. At that moment she had my mother's face. She bounced on the bed and said, "I'm hungry." Then she turned, stared at us and asked, "So, what is it?"

My mother asked, "Where were you?" Her voice was quiet, as if asking the time.

"Oh, out and about."

"It's late. Were you with someone?"

"Yeah, Jack."

"Jack? What Jack?"

"Oh, you know, the guy from the Texaco."

"I don't know a Jack."

And so it went, back and forth, the two of them talking in circles and Father sitting in the shadows of the kitchenette, standing at one point and thundering something about *that guru*, and sitting down again. No one really knew what moved him to action. Perhaps it was Cora's flip response, "Yeah, well, whatever," that drove him across the room in two large steps, his hand raised. But as he swung downwards, my mother, holding her emery board, her knees drawn to her chin, said in a voice calm and hopeful, as if it were a question, "Arnie?" My father stopped. Finally, raising his head and turning to my mother, he said, "Irene, is this what we get? Is this it?" And my sister Cora flinched as if she had actually been hit. The baby began to cry. My father turned and banged out of the room.

After she had calmed the baby, my mother looked at us and said that we were to forget what had just happened. It had never happened before, she said, and it wouldn't happen again. Father was under stress, she said in her soft voice, and she cupped her hands in front of her as if she were offering her children a glance at a rare butterfly, just captured.

I slept in one bed with Amis that night. Cora, unrepentant, slept on the floor between the two beds. My mother sat up with the baby, waiting for my father to come back. I spooned my brother's small body and watched my mother write in a small cloth-covered book she called her journal. I watched the back of her hand slide across the sheets of paper. I watched her heavy chest rise and fall. I watched her mouth chew at her fingernails. I watched the way her knees acted as a table for her book. I watched her with an ache that one feels for a protector, wanting to turn away from her, wanting to call out. Then I fell asleep.

The lights were off when I awoke. I lay still and waited for the room to make sense. I heard my mother whispering and then my father. My mother laughed quietly and their bed moved. It moved for quite a while. I pulled my blanket over my head, and, placing my pillow underneath my crotch, I slowly and quietly masturbated, afterwards falling asleep, empty, placing my cold feet against the legs of my brother.

For breakfast we ate pancakes in the motel restaurant. My father was talkative and relaxed. He didn't say anything about the evening before. My mother too was light-hearted. When we walked back to the room she held my hand and squeezed. I pulled away, feigning interest in something Amis was doing.

By mid-morning my father had retrieved the car. We packed, climbed in, and, as we turned onto the highway, my father said he'd forgotten the warranty for the new rad. He whistled to himself and pulled into the Texaco lot. Jack, the pony-tailed mechanic, was behind the counter, sitting on a stool, smoking. He saw the car and stood, staring out to where we sat, the six of us. My father climbed from the car and walked towards the station. He walked in and leaned on the counter and wagged a finger in Jack's face, pointing back at the car, shaking, pointing.

"Oh, God," Cora said. "Mom?"

"I know," my mother said. "Stay put, will you, Cora? Just stay."

My father turned and left the building. We saw Jack jump the counter and follow. He caught my father by the shoulder and spun him around. It looked so simple when my father got hit, as if the mechanic were slugging a straw man, because my father simply crumpled. But then he stood, brushed off his pants and continued to walk to the car, a strange smile on his face. Jack circled him, bouncing on his work boots, and hit him in the face. My father stumbled, got hit again, and fell. This time he stayed down. Jack kicked him in the stomach. Dust rose from the spot. "Arnie," my mother said. "You bastard." She leaned on the horn and wouldn't get off. Jack looked up at the car, walked over to it, pressed his face against the windshield and stared right at my mother. He didn't look at Cora. Then he pushed away, grinned, gave us a peace sign and walked back to his stool behind the counter.

My mother was still on the horn. I was watching my father, who was now on his knees. He was feeling his face with his hands, trying to rise. He shuffled towards the car and I thought how stupid he was, how proud, and that as I watched him being beaten I didn't really mind.

"What an awful, awful man," my mother said later. We had pulled off to the side of the road a few miles out of Drumheller, and she was swabbing my father's face with a damp cloth. His right eye had swollen shut and he'd cracked a tooth. He lay back against the headrest, his eyes closed, and let my mother nurse him with her soft hands. She prattled while she worked, the kind of thing I'd always liked as a child when I was sick or had taken a bad fall. She kept tipping the thermos full of water onto a cloth, daubing, talking about dinosaurs, recipes she was looking forward to trying, about the lovely rain we would have in Hope. I noticed I was holding Cora's hand; I must have grabbed it at the gas station. It was soft like my mother's, had the same shape of knuckles.

My mother kept nursing my father. She ignored the baby, me and her other children. Her focus was on her husband. She seemed, considering the circumstances, happy and contented, slowly working her way around my father's bruised body. At one point my father sucked in his breath and my mother's lips lifted ever so slightly, as if her goal all along had been to deliver pain. I didn't recognize her then; she seemed older – though more beautiful at that moment than she'd ever been before. But she seemed distant too, cold, turning her back on me, her wonderful hands stroking my father's head, tucking under his chin, her face smiling at his pain. She was a puzzle, a riddle I had no hope of ever solving. Ever.

It was incredibly hot in the car. Tiny buttons of sweat lay on my mother's forehead. Sometimes her tongue curled from her mouth to touch her nose. And at one moment, when she had just finished telling us something unimportant, her mouth remained open and the light struck in a certain way, and a thread of spittle bridged her lips. It shone for a bit and then it broke and disappeared.

HEY

SOMETIMES IN THE EVENING LILY PITCHES TO ME. IT IS the hour between light and dark so I have to strain to see her face; in fact, the blue of her eyes is not there, so all I see are dark holes that flash occasional light. Her arm, a windmill, is a blur, and suddenly the ball is there spinning out of the dusk into my mitt, stinging my palm. I crouch and give her signals, but mostly she can't see them or ignores me and gives me curves, change-ups and fastballs aimed right at my nose. Then it's too dark to see and she yells, "Hey," and ambles towards me. I hunker down and watch her come, small flower, sweat beading on the nose I can't see and, ah, she's there, her crotch level with my face, her loose jeans dusty from a thwacking glove, and she says, "Good. That was good."

She's good; a small woman with a big accurate arm. She puts her medium-length blonde hair up inside her hat and looks like a child. Initially she fools the batters. They get cocky and she gets impish and actually laughs as they go down swinging. I love to watch her pitch and for a split second as she releases the ball she is airborne. She lands with

her head cocked to the left, following the pitch; she is dropping pebbles into a frog's mouth.

She can't hit so I try to teach her. I stand behind her, my
belly on her shoulder-blades, and slow-mo a swing. But she
shrugs me off and says, "I'm a pitcher. I don't hit." Actually,
she thinks it would be sacrilegious to hit off another pitcher.
Sometimes, when the ump doesn't show, I take over and
then Lily gets angry with me. At the end of an inning I follow her with my eyes from behind my mask and watch her
kick a water-bottle or wing her glove at a parked car. In
those moments I think of what great breasts she has, small
fauns, and how I want to share them with the whole world.

I begin to ump regularly. Two games a week. Sometimes
I ump Lily's games, sometimes not. Lily says she's going to
lodge a complaint. She says I'm tougher on her than on
other pitchers. "Your judgement's way off," she says.

"Lodge away," I say, allowing silently that she may be
right. "I call 'em as I see 'em," I add and grin. Actually, the
strike zone in fastball is higher than in baseball and a lot of
people have a hard time grasping that.

Lily knows exactly where the strike zone is and likes to
play the edges. I let her do that a bit but not for a whole
game. "You make a good ump," Lily says. "Just like you
make a good teacher. You love rules." I shrug. Sometimes I
think I like this kind of umping because I'm surrounded by
the turning, milling, sliding and sweating of female bodies.
But I don't admit that. I'm not even sure if that's right.

Lily is studying religion. She has one degree and now she's
going for another. I don't mind this except sometimes I get
tired of teaching just so she can fill her head with Eckhardt
and Brueggemann. I try to be fair but I keep asking, "And to
what end?" I guess what I really want is to move to the sub-
urbs and have a family. Lily says, "No problem, just three
more years."

I take her to open-houses on Sundays and we traipse
around these showhomes that are vast and carpeted and all

look the same. I love their common features, their smell of glue, wood shavings and paint. I pull Lily into the kitchen and show her the European cabinets and their extended hinges. She patronizes me and studies the cutlery drawer. The family room has a fireplace, and I tell her we could install an energy-efficient stove, use the room as a baby room: playpen over there, mobile hanging here. When we leave these places she looks confused. And I am angry. It is in part because of these futile Sundays that quite suddenly one day I decide to leave her.

This day too is a Sunday. My parents are having company, a theologian and his wife, and ask Lily and me if we will join them for lunch. Lily, who has read this theologian and doesn't like him, jumps at the chance. I roll my eyes, bracing for acrimonious table-talk. We arrive and are introduced to Len, a tall, thin, bearded man who bites his nails, and Elsie, who is much younger than Len and has her hair pulled back. She is a tall woman with a stately, young, clean face. During the meal I keep smelling something nice, which I deduce must be Elsie. She strikes me as a woman who wants to be something or somebody she can't. We sit down and my father prays. I watch Elsie, who is staring at her plate.

My mother serves roast beef, baked potatoes and stir-fried vegetables. I am sitting across from Elsie. As usual, my mother is up more than down, running for food. Lily, Len and my father have conquered one end of the table and are talking liberation theology. I remember how Lily, in one of her stages, came to bed with books by Gutiérrez and Echegaray and talked about structures. I pour Elsie some ice-water. She asks, "What do you do, Andy?"

"Teach school," I say. She waits, so I continue. "Junior high math." She nods. I feel small. It's always like that with people like her. I feel I should be a drama prof, a film-maker or even a fisherman for their sakes.

"Do you like it?" she asks.

"I get shit on," I say. I watch her eyes. She doesn't blink. She has big teeth and chews slowly. She wears just a trace of make-up. Len probably doesn't let her use much because that would seem vulgar. I wonder if Elsie notices other men. I wonder if she likes the way I look, is thinking, *God, I love his jaw.*

Len talks about the purification of history and then solidarity. *Solidarity* is a big word these days. It's supposed to mean union, loyalty, respect for others, sharing of wealth, renouncing self, looking after the poor. I once asked Lily who was caring for the rich and she gave me this 'eye of the needle' stuff. I told her, "Right, left, it's all a cesspool of corruption, so don't get your hopes up about changing the world or run off to Central America or something." She called me cynical.

The discussion is heating up at the other end of the table. My father keeps saying "yes . . . but" and getting no further. Lily and Len are talking and no one's listening. I turn to Elsie and ask her what she does. She says she is at home. She smiles. I ogle her teeth and think of riding the bus in high school and the grade twelve girls with their scrubbed faces, their hair pulled back, their widow's peaks, their shine, their blush of expectancy. Elsie looks like that.

I ask, "Do you have children?"

"A one-year-old boy. He stayed in Toronto with his grandma." She wants to talk about him, I can tell. So that is what we do. While Lily and Len spit across the table, Elsie talks to my mother and me about Dieter. Her eyes are oily patches, and she begins to raise her voice but catches and hushes herself. Though she does not say it exactly, she is telling everyone that children are the answer to the purification of history. I smell her as she talks. Surrounded by her, I see her as lost. I see her as wandering in a maze of diapers, God, bottles and Martin Buber. For a moment I imagine myself as her saviour. I look over at Len and laugh inside. He doesn't have a clue. I do. Come, Elsie, I'll rescue you from the clutches of this blind theologian. Does he quote Whitehead as he lies on top of you? Come, Elsie, let's talk about demand feeding, cradle-cap, cracked nipples, the colour of crap.

Suddenly Lily raises her voice and asks Len if he thinks language can save us. My mother looks at my father, who raises his wide hands in the air and says that dessert is ready. Len gives *me* a withering look. It is at this point that I decide to leave Lily. I am suddenly and painfully disappointed in our marriage. Lily is an enthusiast. It's as simple as that. She doesn't hear me. I look at her, she is quiet now, almost sullen, and I wonder, if she knew my thoughts, whether they would be more important than the anaemic man across from her, or language. Right now. I mean, right now. Elsie asks if I would like some coffee and her voice is so soft that I think she has asked me to lay my head on her lap. I say, "Yes."

Of course, I do my usual flip-flop and decide not to leave Lily. She's been pretty nice to me lately; little favours here and there, and when I ump these days she doesn't complain. She just swats me on the bum and says, "Good game," even though we both know I made some lousy calls. I'm realizing too that women like Elsie have weak personalities; that's what Lily said when I asked her what she thought of Elsie. "She may have a beautiful forehead, Andrew, but she's a clinger. She's weak." I don't agree with her wholeheartedly, but I admit she has a needy smell – though I keep it secret that I like that smell.

And then into the first game of the play-offs Lily loses her pitch. She hits a few batters, hesitates in her wind-up, forgets to skip through the windmill; everything about her pitch looks bad. She seems diminished. I watch and try to figure out what exactly is *not* happening; so now, when I ump, my head is elsewhere, and I begin to waffle on the calls and that's no good. One evening after we have practised into the dark and are sitting on our back lawn drinking wine coolers, she says, "I find myself concentrating on the steps: where are my fingers on the seams, how close is my elbow to my body, is my left heel angled enough? I've lost the spontaneity. It's no more fun." She is wearing a yellow tank top and her shoulders and neck glow in the dark. I put an arm around her. She says she doesn't really care about baseball, it just pisses her off that it doesn't feel good any more.

Rubbing her shoulder, I say, "Maybe Augustine has affected your pitch. You should stop reading that old sinner." She laughs; she knows I'm only half serious. Still, all that fall/redemption musing might affect her in some way. The mosquitoes are getting bad, so Lily lights a coil. I rub her neck and she rubs my leg and we smell burnt poison and listen to sirens and cats and later trace each other's jaws with our tongues.

One day I ask Lily if she thinks language can save us and if so from what and do we want saving anyway? She says in some way we all want another life and maybe language can do that for us. So I say, "Thanks a lot, Lily."

She never does get her pitch back. Not that summer. She shrugs and says maybe the talent moved on to someone else. She believes that kind of stuff. Right around this time she gets flushed and frenetic. She decides we need a new cedar deck. She re-sods the back yard. She studies the kitchen and plans to build a nook. She is constantly grabbing at me, holding me, pinning me up against a wall, grinning madly and asking if now is a good time. She drops out of her summer course and stops reading St. Augustine. She says the world doesn't need more people like my father and me. I wonder what she means.

Everything seems hopeful, but of course I keep checking over my shoulder. To me it all feels precarious. I keep on the lookout for rot. I study the elms for tent caterpillars. When I scrape and paint our old house, I look into cracks and holes for termites or decay. I steer away from women with high foreheads. I press my ear into Lily's tummy, as if by doing this I may detect deformities.

I join a slo-pitch team. First base. The rules are different but I'm learning fast. When I bat, the ball comes high, an arc teasing me, begging me to swing earlier, earlier. But the trick is to wait, and wait, and then *crack, give 'er*. This one time when I hit the ball I just know it's gone it feels so sweet. And as I circle the bases I wave at Lily, who's sitting in a lawnchair, fat and happy by the car, but she doesn't see me. She's talking with Glenda – Glenda's almost full term, Lily's only three months – and I realize that Lily never saw my hit. She's leaning forward in her chair, her back to me, and her hands are flying around her face. She's excited, as if all of this, this miracle, this thing happening to us, was her idea.

THE TRANSLATOR

LAST NIGHT, JUST AFTER GOING TO BED, THE telephone rang and for some reason my hands quivered and I imagined it was her on the other end. Though I understood it was impossible, that she didn't even know I was back in Canada, I bit the inside of my mouth, lifted the receiver and waited for her voice. Of course, it was someone else, someone unimportant. I stood in the cold hallway and talked to that someone and then after hanging up I felt this ache in the back of my throat like a cold coming on, so I took two Tylenol and went back to bed.

I met her two years ago in a refugee camp in Thailand. I was working for the Canadian Embassy and I needed a translator. Her name was suggested so I had her called in. She shook my hand when we were introduced.

"My name is Trang," she said.

"Charles."

Her forearms were bigger than those of the other Vietnamese in the camp. Her bum filled out her corduroy pants. Well fed, I thought. I asked her where she was going.

"Nowhere."

"Why?"

"It's my story." She stared. "Do you have a girlfriend?"

"I'm too old."

"You're breaking my heart," she said, textbook perfect, like the idiom of the day. It began to rain. Hard. The tin roof banged and our conversation was halted. I managed to communicate that I could use her. She did not fawn. She simply mouthed a thank you and stepped out the door into a wall of water.

My job in the camp was to check out and recommend refugees for emigration to Canada. Trang was my mouth and ears. In the interviews she sat to my left. Often, I watched her. She had a broad forehead and no crown. Her face was child-like, as if she were still carrying her baby fat. Her hands passed by her face, played in her hair. Her mimicry amused me; that wonderful mouth giving me back my own language. I found myself wanting her. I followed her movements in the office, imagined touching her round nose with my tongue. Like a desperate man I voyaged with her in my head, into dark spaces where a dim light hung over and guided us. It was there I declared my love for her – I had never loved anyone before and having her close to me made me irrational. In the heaviness of the humid night I wanted to bite at her.

When we worked, she was a faithful translator, in the sense she always took on the personality of the speaker: the tics, the idiosyncrasies, the slouch. It was like an art form and this too endeared her to me. At times I did not recognize her. She was an actor telling the most amazing lies. Still, the stories told to me did not move her. I wondered if she felt anything for those people telling their horrific tales. She always managed to stop at the point where she would be personally affected by all of it. After all, she seemed to say, this is a story, I'm only translating.

The United Nations asked me to interview a woman. Her name was Chou. Her papers said she was thirty. She looked forty-five. She was ethnic Khmer but, being from Vietnam, spoke the language, so Trang came along to translate. We went to Chou's house. It was early in May. There was no electricity, no fans, and within minutes my shirt was soaked. I wiped my brow and asked her why she wanted to go to Canada.

"Because my husband is there." She smiled. Four gold front teeth.

"But there is no record of a husband."

"Yes, he went in 1981." She paused, looked at her bare feet and said, "1985."

"Which?"

"1985, I'm sure."

"Do you have children?"

"Yes, sir, three."

"Where are they?"

"One is here, two are . . . " Chou stopped and looked out the window. She shrugged. "Cambodia?" she asked.

"She's asking me?" I said to Trang.

"She doesn't know," she said. I looked over at Trang. She wasn't sweating. She looked forty-five years old. Her face was weathered, beaten. She spread her hands on her thighs. Her hair was tied back with a pink plastic curler. "Thank you for allowing me to go to Canada, Mr. Charles," Trang said.

"Tell her she's going nowhere until she tells the truth," I said. Chou looked hurt. Trang looked hurt. She was wonderful. I dipped back into the dark place with the dim light. I offered it to Trang. "I love you," I said. My audacity amazed me.

"Should I tell Chou that?" Trang asked.

I laughed. "What do you think?"

"I think you are a bitter man and you are scaring me."

Chou mumbled something through an open window and soon bottles of Sprite were set before us.

"Why does everyone want to go west?" I asked.

Trang rubbed her fingers together. "Dollars," she said.
"Love me and you could go too," I said.
"Could I?"

Bitter, she'd said. More like full of spleen, a white face brimming with bile. She didn't say it that way, not with those words, but I caught her meaning. I remembered the story my mother told me, not once but many times, about her family leaving Russia. In the original version she was a one-year-old spirited out of Russia by her parents, who, having watched their factory vandalized and burned to the ground, left the land that had nurtured them for one hundred and fifty years. In another version there was a slight change: she was three years old. Then in subsequent tellings other things changed: her father was tortured by roving gangs of peasants and his hair turned completely white. "Shock," my mother said. I challenged her one time on facts in her stories but she shrugged and said stories evolve, events change, people forget, people remember. "Facts are little things," she said. "Like words."

My mother lived with me until she died. Deadly bricks grew in her breasts. I thought she was young and beautiful. Even at sixty-two. But when I heard Vietnamese refugees telling me why they left their country I kept hearing my mother's voice. And then one day I told Trang my mother was a liar. I began to hate. I was surrounded by deception and disloyalty.

And then a refugee told me his wife had been killed by the government of Vietnam.

"You're lying," I said. "I suggest you turn around and go back where you came from. You've never been married." I had no proof; I was taking a stab.

The man spoke to Trang; his voice went up and down and sometimes sideways. He knotted his pants in his fists. Trang folded her hands and waited. Finally, after a pause, she said to me, "Of all that he said, the following is important: 'You are the emblem of wisdom. May you live to extreme old age, and may happiness always abide with you.' " Trang licked her lips. They shone.

Every Tuesday morning, just after my ice-coffee, Chou appeared at my door for her weekly recital. From week to week her story changed and in my job, if I were to do my job, I needed consistency, facts that hung together, an account that was chronological; not necessarily believable but certainly not impossible. Wrist x-rays showed Chou was forty-one. I told her about the x-rays, certain that she would admit her lie. No, she was thirty. "Why?" I asked. "Why do you insist on being thirty? Say that you're forty-one and I will do something for you. Tell us that you have no children in camp and I will help." Still, she persisted in being thirty, and Boung remained her son. He was twelve. She had him when she was eighteen. Eighteen and twelve make thirty. Trang seemed in total agreement. At the end of one of our Tuesday sessions Trang asked me why I cared if Bun Thi Chou was thirty or forty-one. I rubbed my temples and said, "Achh, achh."

I stayed at camp late one evening and when I was finally ready to leave, I found it was past curfew. Trang told me to wait, whispered from the quad, and returned with a pillow, a towel, a mosquito net and a meal of sticky rice and spring rolls. We locked the quad door from the inside, sat beneath a fan and ate. She sat cross-legged and served me. As we ate she reached out and touched me on my hand, my arm, the side of my neck, as if to say, *You're there.*

Leaving the lights off so as not to disturb the guards, we dipper-bathed beside huge vats of water and slid quietly beneath the mosquito net. Trang fell asleep holding my hands. I lay beside her and listened to an empty country. No traffic, no dogs, no fighting, no noise save an occasional baby's cry or the low shout or grunt of the guards nearby. The guards were lazy. Slept all day, all night. They were little board figures, nothing people in a nowhere place. They had their Mekong whisky, their whores, their now-and-then harassment and forced sex with single Vietnamese women; little slaps to stay awake. No one wanted to run. There was nowhere to go. A woman like Trang, who lay beside me, needed someone white, like me. I could have moved her. I guess I could have taken pride in my power, and of course I did, but there was always the irksome doubt, like a rock in a shoe, that I was being too obvious.

I woke just before dawn. Trang was sitting beside me, watching my face. She was silently mouthing my name. *Charles.* I covered her mouth with my hand. She lay on top of me and made love to me. I remember it that way. She watched my eyes, pulled at my ears, laughed and told me I had beautiful feet. She told me I smelled like a goat and at some point in there I felt that we were alike, that we had suffered equally, we were mortal, we would both live some more and then die. For a few minutes I felt that my body had the same capacity for grief, love and death as hers.

It was curious. When she had finished, she pulled a sarong around herself and went outside. I could hear her bathing. She came back, re-entered the netting and sat mute in the darkness. I reached out a hand to find her and touched her breast. She didn't pull away. Her daytime shyness was gone and I was a little shocked by her matter-of-factness. I felt as if she had just given me chocolates or flowers. I was naïve. As the room grew lighter she told me her story, in order to complete the night. I'd heard the story before, many times from many mouths. "So I gave them my gold and rode in a boat that was old and very sinkable. I came here. Here. I want to go there." As she spoke, Trang kept poking at my palm with her index finger as if to leave a hole there, something to remember her by. To me her story seemed simple, straightforward, so I felt she was lying. I told her that. She added that on the boat she'd cut her hair so as to look like a man. The room grew lighter. As she spoke she pulled at her long black mane. She sat with her back straight. Both legs were to one side, soles facing back. She didn't look as filled-out as when she wore clothes. I found her small, vulnerable, child-like. I pictured Trang and me living in domestic bliss in Canada and I shuddered. I felt tired and fat. The camp began to move. Trang lifted her nose, dressed, touched my forehead and left.

On the day Trang began to work for me the embassy had sent me a young career diplomat, Gerald, to help out with backlog. He came with a vision. He was there to save refugees. He was condescending and very serious about everyone's need for his pity. I disliked his neatly cut hair and his taste for organization and truth. I saw him as dangerous. Too, when I was busy with some menial tasks, he'd spend time with Trang, and Trang said how nice a man he was. I would look at her then and wonder if this was yet another mask she wore or if she really was gullible.

Gerald hated me. Our desks touched and in that small bamboo-walled office we felt each other's heat and ill will. While interviewing refugees I turned my back to him, ignoring his tight-lipped suggestions.

I told him once, "This is not a war we're waging."

He huddled his chin into his chest. "Most of them lie," he said. "Shouldn't we get it right?" Trang heard him but she didn't blink. She was reading the dictionary.

From my office I had a full view of the dusty road leading to the camp prison. The prison walls were corrugated tin six feet high, and every afternoon one of the guards would pull out a slingshot and fire rocks against the tin. The sound was deafening; perhaps because of the intense heat and the lack of shade, sharp sounds became irritants. One afternoon Gerald and I were in the office when we heard shouts, then the banging of rocks against tin, and a guard appeared, cuffing a refugee, shoving him towards the prison. The guard pushed his prisoner ahead, stepped back and began to shoot rocks at the man. He seemed not to want to hit him because the rocks came close enough to the target but never struck. The air was full of resounding booms. The man appeared to be running the gauntlet, dodging, crouching, a cloud of dust enveloping him as he scuffled.

"He can't do that," Gerald said. His lips were pressed tightly together so that his mouth looked like the edge of a piece of paper. Trang, at the side of the room, walked to the cooler and poured herself some water.

"He's not hitting him," I said.

"That's not the point," he said, and knowing he was right I despised him.

"Do something," I said, and then Trang laughed, a soft bubble of noise. She watched me, waiting. Moving away from the window, I pulled Chou's file and threw it at Gerald. "Here, talk to this woman, make some sense of this mess."

The next day Gerald told me the case should be closed. "She's lying," he said. "She's wasting our time." Chou had obviously done or said something to make Gerald set against her resettlement. Perhaps she hadn't deferred quite enough.

"How about the son?" I asked.

"She says he's hers but has no birth certificate. The Bangkok office will do nothing for her unless she has the boy's birth certificate."

I took the file and put it on the cabinet. I looked at Gerald with his clean white shirt and thought, *You don't know shit.* I called Chou in the next morning. She brought me some noodles and a salad. Without hesitating I told her to get the boy a birth certificate. "This is possible so go ahead and do it. Have one made up. If you need money ask Trang. She will tell me." I continued, "You're thirty-eight years old, all right? You had your son when you were twenty-six. Get a proper birth certificate for yourself too. Then come back and see me. Okay?"

Trang conveyed my demands. As far as I could tell she softened the tone. Still, Chou seemed to understand. She looked scared. Trang looked away, as if to say, "And what have you done for me, Charles?"

But it turned out that I didn't have to do anything for Trang. Canada suddenly decided to accept her. She mentioned this to me in passing. "That's great," I said. Acceptance was always assumed to be great. I was a little bit harsh.

Trang looked as if she'd bitten into glass. "Should I write my mother about you?" she asked. The question left me stranded. I laughed and asked if her mother cared. Trang dropped her eyes.

I had nothing else to say. I could have repeated that I loved her but I lacked the vision for that. I watched her back disappear around a corner.

Trang came to work the next day with a pig's head in her bicycle basket. She parked the bike in the shade. The pig's white hairs quivered in the breeze. Every time I passed the bike I was stopped by the stare of the pig. That severed head seemed to be my own. And then, two weeks later, she told me she was pregnant. So, this is it, I thought. It wasn't a lie, because she showed me the OPD test results as she spoke, and her eyes met mine and I said to myself, *This is the truth.* She laid the brown slip of paper on my desk with her light fingers and as she shifted back onto her stool I noticed the outline of her breasts against her shirt.

"When did you get this?" I asked.

"Yesterday."

"Does the embassy know?"

"No."

"You're sure?"

She shrugged. Her nose pinched up at me. I told her to go home and rest, as if she were suddenly an invalid. She did. I sat at my desk and thought how much I enjoyed drinking Thailand's awful-tasting, cheap whisky. When I got home I sat on my balcony and drank half a bottle. That night in bed I felt an ant trail crossing my body so I switched on the light and proceeded to squish the insects, one by one.

The next morning Trang did not come to work. I was grateful. At noon, Gerald sat at my desk and said, "You know she's lying, don't you?"

I wondered where he got his information. I refused to look up from my papers. "That's not the point," I said. In a way it was true. Still, I thought, what was the lie?

Gerald continued, "I just thought it fair to tell you whose baby it was." I looked up, resigned. I didn't feel ready for his revelation. "Do tell," I said.

"Rumour has it, it's one of the guards." Gerald was thumbing his glasses. He was just doing his duty. He was so faithful to his ideas, so rigid. And then, "You should ask Trang. She'll tell you, won't she?"

Would she? My stomach hurt from the heat. I had an infection in my left hand that was working its way up my arm. I wanted to sleep. Instead, in the early afternoon when most of the camp slept, I walked over to Trang's quad. She had her own little room: the floor was covered with green linoleum; calendar pictures of North America were glued to the walls; a small framed picture of an old woman sat on a lone shelf; several articles of wet clothing hung in the doorway. Though I had been invited here before, I had never come. Trang was wearing pyjamas. She had cut and permed her hair. The change shocked me. She had obviously been to see the woman in traditional medicine: her neck was streaked from coining, a process where coins are rubbed on the skin until the blood is drawn out in bruises. I thought it senseless but somehow found it attractive. We sat and sipped cold tea. We said little. I didn't ask her questions. I waited for her to offer me something but she just smiled and touched my hands. I told her I had not slept the night before. She poured more tea and apologized for being sick but said that the next day her head would be better. I studied her face and looked for signs – remorse, deceit, love, anger, passion – but found nothing. She was impassive. I do not know what she saw on my face, perhaps the same. I thought I was suffering.

"How do you like my hair?" she asked. She spoke as if talking past a mouthful of small stones.

"Nice," I lied. It highlighted the acne on her forehead. She no longer wore her pink roller. Then she reached behind her and produced a magazine on Canadian fruit and vegetables. She pointed to a cluster of raspberries. "Good for canning?" she asked. I smiled and nodded. And then she "tssked," something I'd never heard her do before. It was a marmish "tssk," as if to say, *There, there.*

"And these?" She showed me a bunch of cherries.

"Cherries."

"Canning too?"

"Yes."

"Tssk."

For an hour we looked at gooseberries, beans and carrots. I told her she could pickle beets. She didn't know beets. She put a hand over her flat face. I stood. She took my hands and held them to her stomach. Then she handed me a big, black umbrella. "To keep the sun from hitting you," she said.

Her friend Hoa came to see me the next morning. She sat in front of me and said that it would be most good if Mr. Charles had six thousand baht that Miss Trang urgently needed, and could I do that, to be paid back, of course, later. I closed my eyes and leaned back in my chair. I sighed and told her to return the next day. I would have the money. I did not consider. Sloppy, crude methods, danger and risk of death aside, I felt I had little choice.

I was in bed with Dengue fever the next week, and when I was finally able to move I went to Bangkok and flew down to the island of Phuket for two weeks. I slept in an air-conditioned room, swam in the hotel swimming pool early in the morning, went for breakfast, and came back to the hotel and slept the morning away. I slept like death, undreaming, waking up in the same position in which I went to sleep, in my head composing letters to Trang, telling her about the croissants, describing the hot beaches, the bite of God on your shoulders as you lay in the sun. On my fourth night I walked down to one of the beaches and sat in a bar, watching the Thai girls and the foreigners. I ordered a Kloster and observed an older Australian man squeeze the breasts on a sixteen-year-old straddling his lap. The girl serving me was maybe eighteen. "American?" she asked.

"From Canada," I said.

She smiled. White teeth startled me. "I like to go to Canada." She touched my arm. She was wearing tiny black shorts and a tight T-shirt. I could see her belly button through the shirt. She said her name was Goy. "Little finger," she added and smiled. She kept putting bottles in front of me. I got drunk and watched her flirt with other men at the bar. And then I looked up from my beer at one point and she was gone.

I spent the rest of my vacation wandering the beaches, thinking of what I'd become or what I always had been, and I swam in water with dangerous undertow and welcomed the feel of something beyond my control pulling me out to sea. I went home to my house close to the camp and watched the motorcycles roar past my front door. And then I went back to the camp and sat at my desk and people flowed in and out of my office. The heat gave me tremendous headaches. Trang had quit. I found a new translator. His name was Minh and he was much too nice to me. He made a lot of mistakes, but I welcomed those because I wanted nothing to remind me of the perfect translator I'd once had.

I did not see Trang again until the day she left for Canada. She was dressed as though she were going to the mall on a Saturday afternoon. She had on a blue jean skirt with rhinestones, and high heels and pantyhose, and a white top with a Peter Pan collar. She had layered on her make-up, with some kind of funny-looking white plaster over her black eyes. Her head constantly turned as if she were looking for someone. Before she climbed on the bus she hugged me with one arm. I enclosed her and felt her flatness against my crotch, a sadness in my stomach. When Trang was settled on the bus I waved again. The bus left. I went over to the restaurant for a Pepsi, watched a soccer match on TV, and broke toothpicks into tiny pieces. A friend of Trang's stopped at my table and bought me a sweet coffee.

"I don't want a coffee," I said.

"Yes, no problem." He waved a hand at a fly and sat down. "In Saigon City," he said, "I lived across the street from Trang. Close to the river. Tiny street. Stopped street."

"Stopped?"

"Nowhere to go."

"You mean dead end."

"Yes."

Sweat lay on my forehead. I wanted the man to leave. He stayed. He caught flies and let them go. At some point I began to talk. First, about nothing at all. He nodded and pretended to understand. Then, later, I leaned into the poor man and, speaking softly, I told him what kind of person I was.

WHERE YOU'RE FROM

MY BROTHER TIMOTHY CAME HOME TO WINNIPEG ON furlough from Indonesia this past summer.

People would ask him, "Where are you from?"

"The Birdshead," he would answer, and even though he received questioning looks, he did not bother to explain.

He was showing me pictures of the South Pacific, of his compound, the planes, his helicopter, his cook, the beach, and as we looked at the photos a little piece of broken shell fell from between two of the pictures. I picked it up and held it to the light, touching that tiny shard, and I thought, so this is where you're from.

It was a summer of religious hype, or so it seemed. South of us Jerry Falwell was threatening to run for the presidency. *Time* showed George Bush with a skullcap kneeling by the Wailing Wall, and Ronald Reagan with his arm around a priest – just released by his Lebanese captors – saying something about "an answer to a great many prayers." Bush, again, announcing on television that Christ was his personal saviour. And then, a week later, *The Globe and Mail* reported the United Church had adopted the non-sexist words of "father-mother" and "people." Timothy is a great believer, like Ronald Reagan is a great believer. Timothy is a missionary – a bush pilot – who has a small head, big ears, no lips, bleached eyebrows and eyes, perfect green holes that said when we met, *Oh, so this is Canada again, oh.*

In the car, returning from the airport, I looked at him beside me with his hollow tanned cheeks and his bony fingers and said, "You've lost weight."

"Yes," he said.

"The food?" I asked.

"Probably."

"The heat too," I said, offering alternatives.

"Yes, I imagine," he said. He was studying the shops of Portage Avenue as if seeing them for the first time. I looked at him. He wore Hushpuppies and flare pants and a white cotton short-sleeved shirt with one button loosened at the neck. This was familiar to me. When Timothy left years back he was probably wearing this same outfit. He would never admit it, though. However, I will admit that I do not love my brother. I tolerate him. He is too aware of his humility, subtly condescending, as if he knows something ordinary people don't. Worse, he is slowly turning blank, like a man living only in the present (I noticed it first in his letters when he slipped from the past to the present in the same sentence), but this may be because he speaks Dani, which has only one verb tense, the present.

"How's Bea?" Timothy asked. I had to lean towards him, his voice was so soft.

"Good," I said. "Looking forward to seeing you. She still works at Benkhe's part time. Still has dirt under her fingernails."

"She'd love the jungle," Timothy said. He splayed his fingers on his thighs when he said the word *love.*

"Yes, she could rust year 'round," I said. Then I asked him if he had tried the new Coke yet. Maybe because nails gather rust in the old Coke and I've wondered if they do the same in the New Taste Coke, or maybe because I didn't want to talk about Bea and me. Not that we weren't happy. We were – still are – married. Anyway, I said, "Tried the new Coke yet?"

"I'm surprised," he said. "Pleasantly." I was surprised that he was surprised, because I didn't even think he would *notice*. I expected him to harrumph like my father and say, "It's only a drink." He said, "But then I'm so unused to things. I'm not one to judge. Indonesian Coke tastes like your tongue on tin."

"Ha," I said. "Tin Taste, the Classic of Classics. I like that."

Timothy tightened his lips and they disappeared. It struck me that the only thing not tiny on the man were his ears. Elephantine. In fact, my brother's head seemed to have shrunk. I wished for a pair of calipers to measure his head, even to lay his minikin skull on my lap and measure "back and front and every way" like the doctor in Conrad's dark book who eagerly produced his western tool, talking diminishment and changes. But I did not measure. I merely eyed my brother's cranium as a carpenter eyes a plumb-line, with a squint.

Timothy seemed lost in North America. There were no adoring Dani bringing him gifts of potatoes and clams. He couldn't spew Bible verses at Bea and me and, worst of all, he always had his two feet on the ground. He lived for the air. Too, he had missed seven years of our history, important things like Commuter Cups, the death of Mom and Dad, Insta-Bank machines, swivel-head razors.

One day Bea told Timothy we were thinking of getting a ferret for a pet, as a sort of watchdog; it was the latest. Then Timothy said, "One day, my cook Kim goes and eats my dog Leo."

Bea asked, "They do that, eat dogs?"

Timothy shrugged. He was resting his chin on his palm, his elbow on the table. "The Dani like meat," he said.

He got up from the table then – this was two days into his visit and we were in the kitchen drinking Nabob tea and eating crackers and cream cheese – took Bea's heavy red hair in his hands and lifted it skyward, revealing her nape. His fingers twisted her hair and I noticed his thumb pointing skyward.

"If our women saw this hair," Timothy said, "there would be twenty babies christened Bea within the year. They don't understand things like this." He released Bea's hair, patted her on the arm and sat.

Timothy is a soft, nervous man who walks on the thin, crackly pages of the King James Bible without ripping a single sheet. He is – and this is no doubt because of his experience as a helicopter pilot – forever looking above, below and behind him, and in the mornings Bea and I would huddle under the quilt and groan to the sound of floorboards creaking as Timothy rose and opened the window to check the cloud cover, *the ceiling*, as he put it. Morning after morning he repeated the move, always, but unnecessarily, aware of the system up there.

So when he took Bea's hair in his hands, he was out of character and perhaps even surprised himself. Bea too was surprised, but nicely – if only because unlike me she doesn't mind being brushed, jostled, bumped, fondled and caressed. When she first greeted Timothy she threw her arms around him and crushed him so hard his head hung past her neck and shoulder, far enough for me to measure it, though it did not reach my lap. Bea's acceptance of Timothy's touching her was normal; it was Timothy who raised my eyebrows. For someone so keen about his surroundings and his movements – every step seemed torturous – he appeared to forget his position for half a minute and become someone else. After he told us about those future Beas on the other side of the world, his hands reached out again towards Bea, stopped and fell back on his lap. Like the Dani, he was in love with Bea's hair.

When we were alone later, Bea gurgled when I suggested snipping off a lock for him to take back to Irian Jaya, though this is impossible because Bea will never cut her hair. Once a month I trim the ends to keep it healthy; she stands in the kitchen while I kneel behind her, my eyes level with her bum, and *crunch, crunch* goes the scissors. Sometimes I think I married her for her hair, her most beautiful limb, our child. When we first made love I asked her to kneel above me and brush me with her hair from head to toe. Later, when she started working at the greenhouse, she'd come home with dirty fingernails and a smell so earthy and rich it clung to her skin and hair so that at night, in bed, I was unsure whether to water or pick her, and would coax in her ear, "He ploughed her and she cropped," and she'd laugh and pinch my buttock. I have not said that for three years now, ever since the day the doctor clucked and shrugged, waved his chart in the air and pointed a symbolic finger at my stomach. Bea manages fine but I still have this taste in the back of my throat that reminds me of my childhood and evangelistic services. Guilt. This is *your* problem, Thomas; there would be nothing magical in getting Bea to cut her hair – though it has crossed my mind.

My brother always had a sense of mission. I tried to match his idea of purpose and became a nurse. Mom was a nurse. Dad was a pastor. These days I do not nurse, I write stories about my family. My brother says I have lost all sense of purpose. I answer that I do not want to shrivel and dry up like a watermelon seed left in the sun. Mom and Dad are dead. Timothy is my only family.

When we were young, Sunday lunches were spent entertaining visiting missionaries who told stories about the foreign fields. (My mother often said how Timothy, in his prayers, used to ask the Lord to keep the missionaries safe on the corn fields. I must have heard that five hundred times.) One Sunday, when I was twelve and Timothy was eighteen, a missionary couple who had just got back from what was then the Belgian Congo visited our home. The man told us a story. I was sitting beside the missionary's wife, who smelled of damp wool and had bright, bright teeth. We kept knocking elbows while we ate, and I remember wondering what her voice would sound like. What I recall of the man's story is this:

The big question for the missionaries during the civil war was whether to arm themselves. This man had fought hard with the question and finally decided to use his gun, an ancient .303, only if his family's life were threatened. One night he heard a noise in the attic where the grain was kept and, taking his gun, he climbed the ladder to the loft. Hearing scratches in the far corner, he cried, *Come out or I will shoot.* There was no response so he pulled the bolt back, aimed into the corner and fired. The scratching stopped and he crept to where a body lay. It was a young village boy, unarmed, his hand stuck in a sack of corn.

That is all I remember of the story. Timothy would know the details, that being the story that decided his life's goal. All I remember is the man's voice getting softer and breaking as the story neared its conclusion, and the smell of damp wool, and then suddenly the missionary's wife raising her head. Her mouth hung open and the sun, lifting through the dining-room window, struck her bottom lip and her mouth shone brilliantly as if she were hiding gold in there.

I asked Timothy if he remembered that story. We were sitting on the front porch, drinking Extra Old Stock, feeling heavy, and I suddenly wanted to know.

"I remember some man from the Congo who killed a kid," he said.

"Remember his wife?" I asked. "Never said a word. Smelled like wool."

"Don't recall," Timothy said.

"Damp wool," I said, not believing that he had forgotten. He used to kiss the man's shoes, he adored him so. The story had made him weep. "Damp wool," I repeated.

It dawned on me that Timothy did not care to remember. Perhaps because it was too much like returning to one's home town after years of absence and finding everything the same, or because, like me, he realized he had no one to pass things on to; maybe Timothy was beginning to sense the loss of something, the disappearance of a name from the face of this earth.

"Where are we from?" I asked.

Timothy, in step for once, blew up his cheeks and said, "It's not your fault, you know."

I managed a self-deprecating grimace – Bea hates it, she says it's self-pitying. "Bea and I don't apportion blame," I said.

"Bea doesn't," he said.

Suddenly I hated him. "There's proof. Facts. Whatever I shoot out is either dead or quadriplegic. Couldn't swim downstream. Not the end of the world." I looked at him sucking liplessly on his beer. I said, "Got some hocus-pocus for me? Better stick to prayer. I don't like the idea of bat's wings and goat's blood. Anyway, we're getting a ferret."

I was starting to sound silly and bitter so I shut up. Bea came out with more beer and Timothy went upstairs and reappeared five minutes later with his black leather flight bag. Sometimes his timing is awful. From it he pulled a bundle of dried fruit and vegetable shells, long and thin, to which were attached straps and strings. He didn't say anything, and Bea and I just sat there, clutching our beer.

Timothy held up one of the largest shells, about two feet, and said, "Look."

Bea, curious, leaned forward, reaching a hand for the shell. "What is it, Timothy? A water bottle?"

"A gourd," he said. We waited for him to continue. His hands fluttered as he looked for the right words. He said, "They wear it around the waist . . . the men. It's all they wear. As a sign of strength."

"Nawww," Bea groaned. She grabbed the two-footer, fastening it to her waist. The tip of the gourd pointed at the neighbour's chimney. Bea was wearing red shorts and a large white T-shirt tied in a knot at her right hip. She spun suddenly and the gourd swung outwards, narrowly missing Timothy's chin. I laughed and slapped her big thigh, at the same time grabbing for the gourd.

"Don't break it, Thomas," she said, dancing sideways. She loosened the leather straps and sat, droplets of sweat gathering on her upper lip. I could tell by the way she moved her back against the lawn chair that her thick hair was sticking to her wet neck. My hand-print was still on her leg.

"Don't tell me they walk around with hard-ons all day," I said.

"It's a symbol," Timothy said.

Bea asked, "You mean like owning a BMW?"

Timothy didn't respond. He gathered six gourds together and with both hands he stretched them out in offering. "Here," he said, "keep them," and his gesture was sincere, though I sensed a hint of superiority in the giving of this claptrap, like when we were younger and would play sword-drill and he would always win, his thin lips spraying Bible verses around the room while his head swelled from the knowledge of his being right. *Here, take that.* "Here, keep them."

Timothy tipped towards Bea and brushed her elbow with his fingertips as if blessing her, or as if by exciting the down on her arms he could stimulate fertility. I pulled at my ear and remembered Bea and me in our early days, when we were naïvely planning for simple things like children, and how I – I told Bea this – how I would throw my children high in the air, shushing them off to bed, and call out those lovely words, "Shadrach, Meshach and To-bed-we-go."

That night Bea lay on top of me and said, "I really don't know, he was so weird today, Thomas."

"Quiet, Bea, those ears catch all," I whispered, listening for sounds from the adjoining room, not that I really cared if he heard.

"Quiet, Bea," she mimicked, and pulled down my shorts. "Let's," she said, up on her knees so quick the bed groaned.

"Wake the earth," I said, pushing her away from me hard, trying to seem playful.

"Your big brother," Bea said. Her head was turned and her voice bounced off the bedroom wall. "Today we went to

Tim Horton's for coffee and a fritter and he told me stories, like he used to write in his letters, that black magic stuff."

Bea turned her back to me. She propped herself on her elbow and talked to the corner of the room so I could just catch the outline of her lips moving. She has full lips and when she explains something they spread as if she is pouting and her shoulders point upward and inward to her large ear lobes and everything funnels back to her mouth. I love her mouth.

"He told me about a man whose wife died in childbirth," she said. "His tribe wanted him to find out who had used black magic on his wife. This meant taking his wife's hair and smoking it like a cigarette. Whoever gets sick and dies after smoking is the guilty person. No one died so they built a fire on top of this woman's grave and ate a meal there. Again the responsible one should get sick and die. Timothy said a child died, from a swollen stomach. He said it might have been appendicitis . . . but you know, Thomas . . ." She stopped, climbed back on her knees, leaned toward me so that her long braids tickled my chest and continued in a whisper, "Timothy himself seemed uncertain of the child's condition, as if the magic might, just might, have been real." Bea hit my chest hard with her fist. *So there.*

"He couldn't," I said. "He's too aware of sin."

"He could," Bea countered. "That's why he's so thin."

"No," I said, "that's because he forgets. Forgetting dries you up." My chest hurt where Bea whumped me.

"But really, Thomas, it scares me," Bea said. "I like the man, even if you don't, but he's supposed to be giving those people something. I mean, he knows what they need, that's why he's there and we're not." I grabbed Bea then and kissed her mouth shut. Bea is not stupid. She is basically good. In fact, she gives me ballast. While we fell asleep I held her so tight that she said, "My, my," and smiled.

On a Sunday we went to Patricia Beach. Timothy was to leave the following Tuesday. He must have been disappointed with the beach after the purity of the Indonesian coastline, but he said nothing. We found a sand dune which protected us from the wind, and we hid behind bushes and smaller dunes to climb out of our clothes and into our trunks. Timothy was wearing tight bikini trunks. He had tanned arms up to his biceps and his torso was white. He wore a leather thong around his neck, from which hung a tiny metal cross. His legs were smooth, as if shorn, and, watching from my towel on the rocks, I was surprised to see that without his flare pants on, Timothy looked effeminate when he walked. I looked down at my own legs, only slightly hairy, and wondered if when I was naked and walking, my buttocks rolling, I looked like that. I would have to ask Bea.

Bea came out from behind a dune, her orange hair in a pony-tail. All I saw were freckles sectioned by a black bikini. She would burn. "Be careful, Bea," I called to her and pushed my forefinger hard against my chest and released it, leaving a white indentation. "Put on lotion."

She waved her hand, brushing aside my concern, and dashed across the sharp rocks towards the water, the white bottoms of her feet perfect mushrooms.

From the shore I watched Timothy and Bea ride the waves, trying to catch a crest, but it never worked and waves always rolled over and buried them. Observing their play, I wondered where I had been for the last while, why I hadn't noticed them liking each other more and more. But then Bea could do that, make people want her and make it seem natural. From this distance Timothy looked at ease, a child splashing in a tub.

The body-surfing done, they played *horse*, mounting each other's shoulders. First there would be Timothy, his thighs clutching Bea's neck, his own head and shoulders reflecting the sun and, splash, he would fall and Bea would scream. Then Bea was in the air. I could see her shoulders turning pink. I could smell burning flesh. Walking to the water, I waved at Bea as she was straddling Timothy's wet head. She was adjusting her bikini top with one hand and waving at me with the other.

"Come on, Bea," I called as she fell back-first into a wave. I walked to my towel and picked up the suntan lotion. Taking a little in my palm I spread it on my neck, watching Bea and Timothy, who had finished *horse*, diving for the bottom of the lake. They took turns, throwing their heads back for deep breaths and then plunging, their calves and feet twisting in the air, bending, and sometimes, where the water was more shallow, their thighs sitting evident like tree trunks planted in water, Timothy's legs saplings in the wind. Finally, Bea tramped out of the water. Timothy kept diving.

Wringing out her hair over the sand beside my towel, Bea said, "Timothy lost his cross."

"Did you find it?" I asked. Bea gave me a look. "Playing stupid games," I said.

"Go help him, Thomas," she said. "He won't quit till he finds it."

"What's so important about a little cross?" I asked. Standing, I adjusted my trunks. "Put lotion on your shoulders and face," I said and walked towards the water, wondering if Bea still liked my legs. I looked back but she had her eyes closed and was applying lotion.

Timothy was out of breath and seemed a little desperate. "I think it was about here," he gasped. He pointed to the shore. "Even with that tree." Taking another breath, he dived. The water was only five feet deep so I pushed along the bottom with my feet. Warm mud squished between my toes. I dived once in a while, only to soothe Timothy's panic, and rose to the surface with handfuls of clay. After five minutes of this I said, "I think it's lost," and pushed Timothy gently towards the beach. He nodded, his eyes red from the muddy water, and followed me out of the lake. Later, towelled dry, his hair sticking out all over the place, his eyes were green again.

We barbecued pork chops for lunch and ate baked potatoes that had tiny pieces of tin foil sticking to the peel. Then we lay on the beach in the late afternoon sun and I burned my shins. Timothy was lying between Bea and me. I think he slept because his leg jumped occasionally and when he raised his head later his eyelids were puffy. At one point, Bea was spreading lotion on her stomach. A number of blonde hairs sprouted near her belly button. She turned to Timothy, who was lying on his stomach, and spread lotion on his back, starting at his shoulder-blades and moving down to the base of his spine.

"You're burning," she told him.

I watched her hands press into his back. His head was buried in the crook of his elbow. I pushed wet sand and pebbles onto my shins so that the in-between part looked like a miniature mountain pass. Before we left Bea waded out to the spot even with the tree and tried three or four more dives. She got nothing.

On Timothy's final night in Canada, Bea and I attended his last fund-raising service at a Mennonite church in Winnipeg. After the service, in the basement, Timothy introduced us to Grace, a tall black-haired woman whose body whispered when she walked. They had lived on the same compound in Irian Jaya.

"You're no longer there, I understand," I said to her. We were eating butter tarts and holding white napkins. Flakes of crust clung to her upper lip.

"No, I left about a year ago. I guess I'd had enough." She dipped forward as she spoke, as if used to speaking to shorter people. As we talked I watched Bea and Timothy in the far corner of the church basement laughing at a joke. Every now and then Bea reached out to touch Timothy's shoulder. Concentrating again on Grace's face, I wondered if Timothy had ever wanted to make love to her whispering body, lying in the wet South Pacific night while a boa constrictor thumped in the attic above.

Grace came back to our place for tea and while Bea served, Grace and Timothy glowed in Indonesian and let me shield my eyes from a distance, trying to recognize this man who was my only family. As the evening ended Grace walked out of our lives and we said, "Goodbye, Grace." Then the three of us climbed the stairs to our bedrooms.

In the morning we ate a breakfast of boiled eggs and sliced cantaloupe, and Bea and I drove Timothy to the airport. In front of the Air Canada counter Bea held Timothy for ten years and then I kissed him, right in the middle of his small head.

Bea found the house empty and came home with fifteen new plants the day after Timothy left. "What I liked," she said in bed one night, "was that he didn't find us insignificant or silly." She had a fist pushed into my right armpit. Her hair was tied up and shining in the dark.

"Not us," I said. "Just our ideas, everything around us."

"He could have resented us," she said. "Our perfect safety, our unlightenment. Is that a word?"

"He was robbed," I said. "He had no place. But he liked you. Around you he was almost ready to remember who he was."

"I didn't try," Bea said. She fell asleep with one heavy leg draped over my stomach while I lay there watching drool slide from her mouth. She sleeps with her mouth open.

It was a humid night and after a while my body was sticky from the heat. I rolled Bea gently to her side of the bed and got up and stood naked by the open window. The breeze played against my damp skin. I got dressed and then walked outside, got in the car and drove to the 7-Eleven. I bought a Big Gulp and sat on the curb, watching Vietnamese boys hanging around by the telephone booth, chattering, practising ninjutsu on a lamppost. I walked up to them and said, "Boys, boys, where are you from?" and they scolded me in a language that was strange and lovely. When I got home I walked to the storage drawer in the study and pulled out the gourds Timothy had given us. I fingered them, the dry click of their touching the only sound I could hear above the hum of the refrigerator. I thought it might be fun to run naked in the back yard wearing one of these contraptions and call out to Bea through the upstairs window and she would see me, laugh out loud and trip outside to join me. Join me. I clattered the gourds back into the drawer and climbed the stairs to the bedroom. I undressed and crawled in beside this woman lying there. Rubbing the small of her back with my knees, I allowed all thoughts to fade away as the woman's bigness filled my head. It was so nice to drift beside her.

I fell asleep and dreamed that Bea and Timothy had had a baby. I told Bea about it the next day. She laughed.

THE FALL

BUNYAN BEGINS: "AS I WALKED THROUGH THE wilderness of this world, I lighted on a certain place where there was a den (the gaol), and I laid me down in that place to sleep, and as I slept I dreamed a dream. . . . I saw a man clothed with rags . . . a book in his hand, and a great burden upon his back. I looked, and saw him open the book, and read therein; and as he read, he wept and trembled; and, not being able long to contain, he brake out with a lamentable cry, saying, 'What shall I do?' "

My father always thought that my daughter's illness was the wage of some deep-rooted sin, certainly unrepented and probably lascivious; perhaps Candace's and my living together before marriage, or Candace's leaving me just during the months when Anna began to throw knives at her parents. Sometimes, I too wanted to point a finger at Candace and thunder, "This is what you get for leaving me." *You. We.* What shall we do? Blame meanders insidiously. The list: Candace, who admitted to me one night that she

67

did not like her daughter very much. I looked at her and said, "I know." My father, who hammered nails into me with spine-tingling tales of the Apocalypse. My mother, who lived a separate life, always physically present but with her head in a different world, inventing her own ways of escaping her husband's visions. The doctors, stymied by the complexity of Anna's brain. And my own hands, which had tried so hard to cup and protect my child's head and failed, because the palms were too small and the girl too quick, the laughing head too elusive. And, finally, blame ended up on the floor. Dustpan material.

As a toddler Anna was clumsy, as toddlers tend to be, and she'd sometimes fall and hit her head on the concrete basement floor. It was a soft, delicate sound, like a pumpkin dropped from a short distance onto marble; the sound itself was so pillowy and unimpressive that it was grotesque because I knew, every time I heard it, that concrete does not forgive. The first time Anna fell in this manner she was standing on a tricycle seat and she fell backwards, straight out, not curling her body. Her arms flung backwards, but she never made the instinctive fold and drop to her bum to cushion the fall. Candace was upstairs doing her nails and I had been lying on an old couch watching Anna play, smiling at her through sleepy eyes, and when I opened my eyes she was pirouetting on the tricycle seat. After the fall Anna began to cry and then stopped. I picked her up. She was stiff, as if she'd had the wind knocked out of her, but I knew her head had taken the brunt of the blow. When Anna began to shudder and roll her eyes I called hoarsely for Candace, who ran down the stairs, cotton batting set between her toes. Anna was the colour of cold steel. As I handed her to Candace, she began to breathe again. "How'd it happen?" Candace asked. Oh, the accusing tone. I would have done the same thing.

"I turned my back and she fell off the trike," I said.
"What'd she hit?"

"The side of her head," I said. "Right side." I touched the spot. Standing there, I thought my lie was the perfect size to fall between two of Candace's painted toes.

Within the next month Anna fell two more times with the same results. So the tests began: EEG, Catscan, MMR. Hospital offices and rooms began to seem like a maze from which we would never be released – a labyrinth of corridors and tunnels filled with lunch carts and white-gowned orderlies and death and limbs and insides and outsides. The doctors found nothing. No soft spots of the skull, no obvious blood vessel on the edge of the brain waiting to explode, no evidence to nod at and say, "Here, this is our problem." Just hunched shoulders, sidelong glances and guilty eyes glazed by doubt. But Anna became more stable and stopped falling, so our doubts and fears dissipated, although sometimes, watching a football game, I'd shiver when the punter's foot popped into leather.

A child's world is limited to kneecaps, table-legs, forbidden stairways, sticking doorknobs, early bedtime and the prospect of looking up only to see chin bottoms, roofs of mouths, yellow incisors and the occasional glance downwards as the child looks up and screams. *Up.* Anna may have refused to accept that she lived in a limited world. She was both frustrating and frustrated. One time, just after her third birthday, during one of her tantrums, she pointed a finger and told me to leave. "Get the hell out of here," she said, and when I stepped closer to corner and hold her she bellowed and threw herself against the wall. I walked downstairs and told Candace our daughter was demented. That same night I crawled around on my hands and knees for two hours, trying to see Anna's world. I got sore knees.

Like my father I look for cause and effect. When, at the age of five, Anna walked through the doors of the children's psyche ward for two weeks of testing, I thought back to the December evening when she teetered and fell off the trike.

In a way I was comforted by my conclusion. I had something with which to explain her illness. But I could not tell Candace because she had left. "I need some time to think," she'd said. Candace did not run off with another man. That, in fact, was probably the farthest thing from her mind. She was leaving a child who would have no more to do with her and a husband who was concentrating more and more on the child. It was a vicious circle. The more Anna rebuffed, the more Candace withdrew, and the more I dived into that little life and was accepted.

I went to pick up Anna after her two weeks of tests. It was thirty-five degrees below and I wore a down parka, felt-lined boots and thick mittens. Anna was waiting for me at the front door, her nose pressed up against the glass; a ward-worker stood off to one side, smoking. Anna looked at me with hard eyes and then smiled as if smirking at my bulky parka. Or maybe she knew already her mother was gone. I hit my mittens together. Again. "Are we ready?"

"Ask Johnny," Anna said, thumbing back at the smoker. Johnny nodded and said the doctor would call the next day. In the car Anna sat with her legs ramrod in front of her. She was carrying foam hospital slippers. "I like these," she offered. "They go puff when you walk." Our tires squeaked through the turns till Anna said, one hand on her hip, "And, how sick are we?" I flinched, hearing my own voice. Anna was wearing tight jeans and a loose T-shirt that said *Just Say No* on the front. Her parka was unbuttoned and hung off her like an unwanted rag. She refused mittens. She was five. She looked fourteen.

"I haven't talked to the doctor," I said. I wished Candace was there to take this girl's wrath. I preferred mopping up after. Back home Anna hit the TV button and watched reruns until she fell asleep. She was fairly docile. I figured they must have had her on something.

Ritalin for breakfast, the doctor said. "Is that necessary?" I asked, hating the sound of the man's nasal voice on the phone. I pictured him with his chalky face and hands softer than Downy-laced towels.

He was in a hurry. "Anna's repressing something," he said, as if that were enough.

"So, drugs," I said.

"I'm not sure if this is the time for cynicism," the doctor said. He was testy. Clearly, he knew little more than I did.

"What about the falls when she was young?" I asked. "Is there a connection?"

"A soft skull?" It seemed a joke and I realized that nothing could be that simple to this man. I regretted sharing my daughter with him. "The medical tests don't show evidence of that," he continued. "I'll have to see you today and explain drug doses and so on. Also, I'd like to talk to you and your wife. That would be helpful."

"My wife ran away," I said, cringing. I could see the raised eyebrows.

"Oh. Well, do please try to see me. Or someone. You know?"

Do I know? Some things. My father is bald, I am bald, and fortunately for Anna, she will not be bald. But there are other things besides genes that skip merrily into our systems. I have thought of throwing out the TV, of taking Anna off sugar, of repenting, of putting my fist in her face. One night Anna saw Candace and me making love on the living-room floor. We thought she was sleeping and then heard a voice on the stair. "What are you doing, Daddy?"

"Wrestling," I said.

"With no clothes?" she asked. And then, "What's wrong with your penis?"

Candace wrapped a black robe around herself and guided her back to bed. She came back smiling, snapping her fingers at me, saying, "What's wrong with your penis, Donald?"

Candace sent a postcard. She wrote about trolley cars and great French restaurants and warm air. I read the card to Anna. She had just showered and I had put her hair in braids – sort of – while we sat in front of the TV watching a basketball game. Anna said, "She's such an asshole sometimes."

"Oh," I said. I wasn't feeling strong enough for a fight. The part in her hair was crooked but I left it. Her mother would have re-done it.

Anna laid her head against my chest, perked her tiny nostrils and asked, "Is Candace unhappy?"

"What do you think?"

Anna picked at an eyebrow. With her hair done she looked so pulled together, incapable of flying apart. *Snap.* The week before Candace left, Anna wrote *I hate you* with her own shit on Candace's mirror. "I will not put up with this sickness. I cannot," Candace hissed at me that night. Her eyes were black, her mouth agape, and she had her head tilted at me as if asking, "Whose child is this?" She was already pregnant with our second child, although we didn't know it, but I should have guessed because she looked fuller; even in that despairing state she carried herself proudly, as if she had to prove that Anna was an aberration.

Candace was still gone when my mother called from her home in rural Manitoba and said it was time for her to die. So Anna and I drove across the prairies to visit Anna's melodramatic grandmother. The trip was a cold one and required frequent breaks in truck stops where Anna ate grilled cheese sandwiches and I drank black coffee and we talked about being truckers and Anna said it would be great, just great, to sit way up, like being on a cloud. I remember thinking that Anna would never make it, unless drugs pulled her into old age. At one restaurant in Indian Head a young truck driver with red hair stopped at our table to chat and Anna told him she liked his belt buckle. After the redhead sat he kept looking at her from his counter perch. Later, in the car,

Anna worked away at Liquorice All Sorts while I turned dials, looking for radio stations. She asked, "How come only men drive trucks?"

"Not so," I answered. "There are women truck drivers too."

She wanted to know why she had never seen a woman truck driver before and if they were fat too, and did truck drivers get married and how come that redheaded man back in the restaurant kept looking at her? I didn't answer. I wondered where Anna had learned to flirt; it was the way she perked her head, came back at someone with eyes spanking, and the way she talked, like someone much older. She was never that way with me, nor with Candace. Certain situations, certain people sparked her. I remembered when my brother visited a while back and he and Anna had been in the basement for what seemed forever, and then they'd come giggling and running up the stairs to the supper table and I'd thought, how nice to hear Anna laugh. Driving down the Number 1 highway, I said to her, "Has anyone ever tried to touch, like, you know, your vagina?" She watched the road and didn't answer for a while and then said, "I don't know, never, I think, what do you mean, exactly?"

I waved a hand, blushing, which was silly because I'd been on the verge of cause and effect and I could have pushed it, demanded to know if Peter had ever put his hand in her panties, or if a worker at the nursery school had fondled her, but it scared me. What if nothing had happened? I was getting a headache from driving. I stopped the car on the side of the road and kept it running while I snoozed and Anna played I Spy. I fell asleep and dreamed that blood was running from my ears.

Candace could have lived with the tantrums, even the knife-throwing. She kept saying, "It's healthy, no one will be better balanced than Anna." But with the shock of the message on the mirror she could no longer rally her strength, and she decided that her daughter was forever lost. She told me so the night she left. She leaned on the door-jamb, hands joined to her coat pockets, and asked how Anna could possibly be her child and what kind of a monster was she and the only worse monster in the world was her own mother because she was leaving. And then she left, her shoulders looking large and significant beneath her coat. Candace, tough and tightly coiled, can outwrestle me and pin me to the rug with her crotch on my neck and make me say *uncle*. Her body is sweet and hard, like candy. Anna has her mother's body. In fact, driving across the country, I had to keep telling myself it was my daughter in the passenger's seat and not my wife. They smelled the same.

My mother was not dying. She'd had a bad attack of gas and thought it was a heart attack. My father sat at the kitchen table cracking peanuts, telling us this, shaking his shiny head and saying only Emma could mistake flatus for a heart attack. Anna's eyes were as wide as her forehead, taking everything in: the setting, the conversation, the brown blotches on my mother's arms, my father's belly. This is what I saw. My mother gave me coffee and Anna apple juice and said we must be tired from the trip. She pointed her chin at Anna as if to say, *So, this is the sick child.* Anna said, "We're truck drivers. Inimitable." She spoke slowly, pronouncing each syllable, and stuck her lips at her apple juice. My mother and father looked at her.

Peter came home, thumped the snow off his feet and rubbed his hands briskly as he entered the kitchen. He stared at the back of Anna's head. "Hey, hey," he said, "the prodigal," and he smacked my shoulder. Anna kept her glass at her mouth, staring sideways at her uncle from inside her juice. "Mom does have power, doesn't she?" Peter said, crushing a peanut between thumb and forefinger.

My mother asked, "How was church, son?" and then, not waiting for an answer, said that Anna and I would sleep in the twin beds in the guest room. She raised a finger and pointed behind her. Between the index and the middle finger of her left hand was a groove left by years of holding a pencil and writing letters to the editor of the local newspaper. Her letters were not political or moral, but pointed out errors she had found in the latest issue. She would read with a red pen and scissors in either hand, and stroke and snip, blissfully unaware of content, her hawkish eyes greedy for mistakes. She was good. Every day found her in her old green Lazy Boy, chortling at dangling participles, missed possessives or, wonder of wonders, a mixed metaphor. My father read the paper to glean hard evidence for the second coming.

My mother was a sixth-generation Swiss Mennonite who fell in love with a first-generation Russian Mennonite. She was to have supper on the table at six o'clock sharp. All her life she alternately shouldered and fought against her chosen fate. "This town is parochial," she'd say to my father or to anyone else who was willing to listen. On her sixty-fifth birthday she decided to take back her maiden name: Martin. My father, stung, said, "Me a Block, you a Martin, what will the church think?"

"What about you?" my mother replied. My father didn't answer. He hid away in his study and then came out and announced that he would forgive my mother; I think not because she was right, not because he loved her, but because to forgive her was the best way of making her feel guilty. My mother accepted forgiveness, and then I imagine she adjusted her silver glasses, raised her thin lips in a half-smile, and kissed my father on the brow.

My mother a bit of a snob, a result of her misunderstanding of small-town people who spoke Low German. She is also, even after thirty years in Canada, quite American – born in Kansas. She takes a lot for granted and assumes that what she says or does, or even how she votes, has little to do with life outside her little kingdom. I thought she'd be a great remedy for Anna.

Two days into our visit, my mother said, "You don't talk to her enough." Anna was outside playing with Turtle, a low-slung cocker spaniel whose teats drew tracks in the snow when she walked.

"We talk," I said.

"And Candace, did you two talk?"

"We still do," I said. "She's coming home." I winced. The night before I had listened to Anna's drug-filled dreams and begged God to kill my wife, absurdly believing that this would be the only thing that would save my daughter.

"You have to learn to cajole," my mother said, squeezing a dishrag and slapping at a fly on the windowsill. "All my life I've cajoled your father."

"Something I've never learned to do," I said.

"Exactly."

The day before, Anna hadn't come to the table when she was called to lunch and I found her lying on the bed, her left hand a visor on her forehead. "What are you doing?" I asked.

"Lying in the corn," she said. I was standing over her and her eyes shone like golden-kernelled nuggets. "I'm a bug," she said, and then continued gentle as ever, "and you're the fucking friendly giant."

"You want to go home?" I asked.

"I don't like Peter, he's a fag like Mr. Rogers."

"Isn't Mr. Rogers dead?" I said, and reached out a hand to drag her from her bed.

"No, he's not, Mommy is." She touched her nose with her tongue. "Can you do this?" she asked. I turned and left.

Candace located us by phone that same night and announced, "I'm pregnant." Her voice was light, hopeful.

"How do you know?"

"I *know*."

"Is it mine?"

"Of course."

"Should I tell Anna?"

"I don't know."

"Always *don't know.*"

"It's Anna, she makes us unsure of things."

"Are you coming home?" I asked.

"Sunday. She's my *daughter*, you know. We have to live together. I'm not a shit."

"I know."

"Everybody says so, don't they? *That's why she's sick*, they say. *Because of her mother.* Right?"

"No, no, not right. Anyways, who gives a damn about these people, this town. Anyone here who's gone bankrupt or is mentally ill or has bad teeth must have some unconfessed sin. God has not blessed us, Candace."

"Oh, but we are blessed, Donald. I see that now." She sounded so enthusiastic that I sighed and told her, "Be good."

I did not tell Anna about the baby. I didn't wish to plumb those depths. I was getting a sense for her I'd never had back home. At night she'd cry out from bad dreams and I'd crawl under her quilt to comfort her and stay there the rest of the night, feeling her sharp elbows, her soft heels, her broad back as she flailed and slept, thrashed and dozed, and woke in the morning, a tiny leg thrown across my hairy back. I loved her. Like a wife – because I hated her too. Hated what she was doing to me, killing me. During those nights I'd lie still and when her pummelling stopped I'd draw her close and press my nose to her hair and wonder how a head so confused could smell so sweet. I wanted her to sleep forever beside me, I wanted to cover her face with a pillow. Sleep.

On Saturday morning, eating breakfast before packing the car to leave for home, Anna said, "I hate goddamn Shreddies," and threw the bowl against the wall. She beat the table with her head until I reached over and clasped her rigid body and squeezed it against my chest.

"Anna," I hissed. She threw her head backwards and caught me on my bottom lip, splitting it open. Blood dripped onto her T-shirt. I carried her to her room and pinned her to the bed until she fell asleep, her body curled into itself.

My mother stood crying in the kitchen, pouring me coffee. "Too much, too much," she kept saying. I dabbed at my swollen lip and stared out the window. My mother said that we should stay, that Anna was not fit to travel. I shrugged, studied her age spots, drank coffee.

Anna woke up late in the afternoon, cheeks hot, sweat on her brow, complaining of a headache. I gave her Tylenol. We said goodbye to her grandma and grandpa and drove into the beginnings of a blizzard.

"Great," Anna breathed, watching the big stars splash our windshield. An hour later the fields and farmhouses on either side of us were obscured by a white wall. Few cars were left on the highway. We stopped at a small hotel for the night. While we ate fish and chips in the empty restaurant, Anna's eyes were wide and clear, the whites meringue like the snow. Back in our room, she kneeled on the bed and pressed her tongue against the window. I unpacked a suitcase and pulled out *Pilgrim's Progress*. It was the same book my father had read to me as a child, and I'd found the battered copy at home and slipped it into my bag.

Anna tired of the storm and curled up in front of the TV. Thumbing Bunyan's testament, I remembered, with a sharpness in my neck, the day I'd become a Christian. My sole intent back then at the age of six had been to emulate Christian, to join him on his trip to the Celestial City. The journey had its own intrigue, and I had been wonderfully lost in a world of mire, fiery darts, sloughs, hapless, deceiving comrades, and the burden, and, suddenly, the magical unloading of that same mass. It was real.

My father fell once. The spring I turned fourteen I was helping him remove the second-storey storm windows. I held the ladder while he climbed gingerly to tap-tap at the clasps. At one point he asked me to fetch a screwdriver. As I returned, running around the corner, tool in hand, I saw my father reaching for a window that was just out of reach. The ladder slid and my father fell. Midway he looked at me and his eyes seemed to say, "What shall I do?" He broke his arm. All my life I have lived with a religious image of falling. In many ways I still have a child's inability to distinguish between metaphor and reality. I lie down in my den and dream dreams of women with babies, children and old people, all with mouths wide open, falling, their eyes asking what to do.

Anna slept. I touched my hand to her back as if stroking her burden. My hard wife was hurtling through the air in another country. All sense of the outside world was cut off; the blizzard had broken telephone contact, the TV was black and the radio was a cackle of static. The room was nondescript. We could have been anywhere. Or nowhere. I undressed Anna and slid her under the blankets. I stripped to my shorts, brushed my teeth and lay in bed. My feet were cold. I slept fitfully, aware that my palm lay on the side of Anna's head. We woke to a white universe. During breakfast Anna fingered her halves of toast. "When's Mommy going to have the baby?" she said.

"Who told you?"

"Grandpa."

"Not for a long time," I said. I felt sorry for my father.

"I like babies," Anna said. Jelly ran down her chin. She brushed at her forehead with the inside of her forearm.

The highway was empty; a black, icy line going straight through the country. There were few cars. Graders, snowploughs and salt trucks crawled through the snow. Anna bounced lightly from front to back in the car, oblivious to the treachery outside our metal cocoon. In a small, desolate place I phoned Candace and told her we'd be home in six hours. She asked, "And Anna?"

"Yes," I said. "Okay."

"Has she said anything about me?"

"Hasn't said much of anything. She's okay."

"I'm scared," Candace said.

"I know."

"She's breaking my bones," Candace said.

When Anna was in the womb, Candace and I would make love and Candace would complain that I was too heavy, so we would either roll over or I would raise myself on elbows and knees so I felt like someone praying over a mountain. "Lessening the load, Candy," I'd say.

"You're still breaking my bones," she'd say, though I was barely brushing her skin. After Anna was born she stopped complaining, let me press her against the sheets, smiled with her eyes closed and claimed I was light.

"Don't let her hurt you," I said.

Silence and then, "Tell her it's lasagne for supper."

From the store where I was calling I could see Anna's head above the dashboard. At this distance it looked as if she were standing on the seat and fiddling with the radio dials. She glanced over at me. I waved. She must not have seen me because she didn't respond. Just kept staring. After Candace hung up I held the receiver, watching my daughter, who still seemed not to have seen me. It was as if she'd suddenly discovered her father and mother were elsewhere, that most people were elsewhere. She didn't flinch. She stared out the cracked windshield, hunting me down. She would always do that, hunt me down. I realized then, with a goosey shudder, that I would always let her find me.

SITTING OPPOSITE MY BROTHER

TIMOTHY MARRIED AN AMERICAN WOMAN WHO WAS really Guyanese and he moved to California where he taught prospective pilots how to fly. He phoned me once and said, "We try to simulate the dangers someone would encounter in Irian, although here we have no airstrips hewn out of the mountainside and the weather patterns change more slowly. This is California. But sometimes we go up to Idaho where the terrain is rugged."

His voice came to me clearly, as if we were young again and sharing a bedroom, our voices floating around in the dark. Once I thought I heard his wife in the background and I asked, "How's June?"

"Good," Timothy said.

"And Sunny?"

"Oh, Sunny is wonderful. A big bright light." He whispered as if what he was telling me was too valuable to spread around, or as if he was worried about my feelings.

"What, nine months?" I asked, and then before he could answer, I asked him if he missed Indonesia. He didn't respond to that, either, but talked excitedly about the two pools in their apartment block and about June finding part-time work. As he spoke I thought of June and, remembering a photograph of her and how the sunlight fell on a dark, sculpted neck, I imagined her sitting beside – no, lying in the same bed as my brother, casting this big, black shadow on a man who had always wanted to shine; the way we used to sing, "Jesus bids us shine with a clear, clear light."

What worried me was that little tawny baby of nine months. Bea and I had pictures of Sunny on our fridge. I tapped at them with a lecturing forefinger and said, "Look, Bea, not a speck of resemblance to my brother. He's been taken."

"Humbug," my big wife announced. "You're jealous, and anyways, Thomas, it's none of your business."

"Well, don't you think Timothy would like to know?" I asked. "He's obviously blinded by something." I stooped to a photo of black black June holding aloft a little brown loaf, as if offering it for a sacrifice. "He has June's chin, nostrils, eyes, lashes. He has small ears, a big mouth. Nothing of Timothy's. Unh, uh," I concluded. "Not a speck."

Since my brother had returned from overseas and married, I found I still did not know him. Did not understand him. We rarely spoke and when we did he was quick to point out his accomplishments. Even this Guyanese woman seemed a trophy of sorts.

"Why?" I asked Bea. "Why would he live with the people of Irian Jaya for twelve years and then marry someone eight thousand miles away?"

Bea took my face between her palms. "Maybe he loves her," she said. "And besides, she's lived ten years in the States." Simplistic, I thought. I watched Bea's neck move as she called me trite, desperate and a rumour-monger. She put her arms around me and I felt the push of her cheekbone on my chest, her stomach against me. She was gaining weight, becoming pudgy, losing the tightness she'd had since we first

met. Sometimes I minded, sometimes I didn't. I squeezed a
roll on her waist and pressed our hips together, my hands
levering her bum. She grinned and jabbed me with an elbow.

June wrote a long letter; using Blake, she poked fun at
Timothy's beliefs: "We both read the Bible day and night /
but he reads't black where I read white." (I thought, ah, the
vestiges of a colonial education. Timothy had said she was
educated in a private school – her parents had been
diplomats.) She spoke of Timothy as being sweet and pre-
cious. Then she asked Bea and me to join their family in B.C.
for Easter weekend. I said to Bea, "This woman is a gift to
us. Where did Timothy find her?"

Bea and I flew to Vancouver, and as we took off I ex-
perienced the usual tautness in my abdomen and then, level-
ing off, the exhilaration of still being alive; the brief thrill of
living in a constant state of grace. We rented a car and drove
up to Whistler where Timothy and June had already settled
into the master bedroom of our rented condo. When she
met us, June reached up and gave Bea a kiss, then me. She
smelled of perfume. I wanted to touch her hair; it was rowed
and beaded and sculpted. She had a long face and a long
torso. Her legs were short. She was wearing a black sweater
and skirt, no stockings. Timothy came around and put his
arm over our shoulders, Bea's and mine. He smiled thinly;
his face was as I remembered it, gawky and bleached. His
teeth were thin and spaced. He looked at Bea, lifted his right
shoulder as if shrugging off a fly and said, "Bea, you look
great." He dropped his eyes as if he were maybe lying, but
Bea merely pushed up her nose in thanks.

"So, where's the little guy?" I asked, and then we were
in the bedroom looking into the playpen at sleeping Sunny,
and standing there I had the impression we were, the four of
us, at the rim of a well, looking down one hundred and fifty
feet into a black pool where a little burnished jewel bobbed
and floated.

"Sundeep. Sundeep Knowlton Felix. But we call him Sunny." June was sitting at the table by the bay window which overlooked the road winding down towards the village. She was filing her nails and telling us about her family. I wanted to ask how Timothy's last name fit into all this, but I held back and stared at June's long fingers. She was young, younger than her pictures showed. Also, she wasn't completely Americanized. She had a good vocabulary but she tended to stress syllables unpredictably – when she said my name her voice lifted at the end. I found the music of her speech intriguing. I wondered how Timothy had ever managed to marry her. He seemed so tiny in her presence. Later, I realized this was exactly the impression he wanted to give.

Timothy and I went for a walk. He pushed the stroller and I walked beside him, our feet kicking pebbles off the asphalt, both of us breathing steam and not talking. We walked down among the shops. There were two rows of cedar buildings with a cobblestone centre courtyard. We found a bench and sat. The sun was shining on Sunny's sleeping face so, to protect him, I backed the stroller into the sun. At one point I brushed shoulders with my brother and he said, "June has strange dreams. Well, not dreams exactly."

"What? Visions?"

"She doesn't think they're dreams and they've only happened twice. Abductions," he concluded, suddenly lifting his head and trying to look up the mountain. I waited. "Check with her," he added. "I don't know if she wants me to say anything." We stood and began to walk again. Timothy had aimed the stroller at the curb and Sunny bounced and squealed.

"I'm curious," I said, hopping onto the sidewalk, pulling in close to Timothy. "Why June?"

"You mean, why did we have to marry?" Timothy asked, his blue eyes bright with sincerity.

"No, not exactly that. It's just, she doesn't fit."

"But we do fit," Timothy said. "She came to me and

said, 'Timothy, you are a strong, responsible man,' and so I did what I had to do."

"Knowing Sunny was yours?" I asked, immediately ducking my head at my own question. Timothy stopped and swivelled. His face held an earnestness mine will never attain. He is a serious, unblasphemous man and, at that moment, he shamed me.

He asked, "What are you saying, Thomas?"

"You're lucky," I said. "She's lucky. Everyone's lucky." I squeezed his elbow, jarring him with the touch, and then I swung an arm at the view. "Nice, eh?" I said.

That evening we ate Pflinzen stuffed with peaches and sour cream. June pronounced them wonderful. Timothy mentioned that it was the day of Christ's crucifixion and we all nodded, Yes, indeed it was. At that point June tore into her story of her abduction by aliens at the age of thirteen. I caught Bea's eye and smiled as June's voice trilled out how she was captured by extraterrestrials, short little men, and how a long metal scoop was pushed into her stomach and her ovum was stolen. "I still have the scar from the scoop mark," she said.

June stood and lifted her sweater, pulled at a matted slip-like undershirt, and pointed at a spot to the left of her belly button. I strained to see the scar she was fingering, but found myself mesmerized by her skin and the edges of her lower ribs peeking out from under her sweater. "Hmm," I said.

Bea reached out and brushed the tiny spot. She asked a question but I didn't hear it. I was shocked by the deathly flush of Bea's hand against June's stomach. Bea's freckles, to my mind, looked like a skin disease; I saw a mottled, bleached and ugly limb belonging to my wife. I poured myself some wine and drank quickly. June sat down and dived back into her tale.

"Then, a few years later, I became pregnant. Quite mysteriously. There was no way I could have been pregnant, yet my stomach actually began to distend, and then at four months it stopped and the pregnancy disappeared. Two years after that I was once again abducted by the same short people. They showed me a child who had a sickly pallor, was white, white and very small, and they said it was my child." June touched her lips to some wine. She held her goblet (for this is what it seemed – it was a big piece of grey stoneware) as one holds a boulder about to be thrown. "The whole situation was unnerving. Ridiculous. Yet I couldn't put it off as just a dream. It had been too close, too real, especially given that I was pregnant and showing."

Bea asked, "Did you test positive?"

June shook her head. "I never tested myself."

I thought, hysterical pregnancy. June looked up and said, "Some would say 'hysteria', but that's just the simplistic response of non-believers."

She swung her hand abruptly and for a second I thought she meant to hit me, but she picked up her goblet.

Later, as June and Timothy got Sunny ready for bed, and Bea and I cleaned up, I leaned into Bea's neck, chuckled and said, "Funny, but tonight I realized they deserve each other."

Bea pulled away. "That sounds malicious," she said.

"Not at all." I rested my chin on the top of her head and pressed down. Hard.

"Don't, Thomas." She shook me off. "You're such an ass sometimes."

I dropped my jaw and feigned hurt. Of course I shouldn't have expected Bea's support. In the last year she had discovered dreams, become fascinated with them. She had trained herself to wake up and record them. Many a night I rolled over to find Bea scribbling, her book and spotted hand caught in the yellowed halo of light, her shoulder-blades pointing back at me through her thin top. I would close my eyes and look for sleep, but her pen scratched at the backs of my eyes. By her bed lay the great thinkers on dreams, and one night I leaned over and read, "A. dreamt of *seeing a former governess of his in a dress of black lustre ('Luster')* which fitted very tight across her *buttocks*. – This was explained as meaning that the governess was lustful ('luster')." And farther down, "A man dreamt that *he was a pregnant woman lying in bed. He found the situation very disagreeable. He called out: 'I'd rather be breaking stones.'* "

I read more. Though I neither understood nor believed everything, I enjoyed it. I marvelled at the imagination involved, at how everything came back to sex, at how some of what I read related to my life, to Bea. I closed the book. Finding sleep impossible, I panned for blackheads on Bea's back, telling her to lie still when I found one: how curious they were when encouraged to exit, spilling out a tiny purple seed the shape of sperm. I mounted three of them on my forefinger and curled the gold around to Bea's face. She said, "Aw, yuck," and resumed her writing, her back a wall, her hair a bloody drape I wanted to rent. I recalled with some self-pity recounting my own dreams long ago, dreams of her and Timothy having a baby, and her laughing in my face.

June was likeable. We sat around the fire in the evening, eating Purdy's chocolates and drinking white wine; Timothy drank ice water. June was barefoot, as was Bea, so I played peekaboo with their feet, smiling at how June's arches climbed to the sky, curved on forever and then dropped to her narrow heels where the faintest trace of callus ran around the edge. Bea's feet I liked too, but they were familiar and chaste. I liked the hue of June's insteps, her heels ripe sloe, the smooth rise and fall, two dark flowers growing earthwards.

Timothy, pushing at an ice-cube with his thumb, was telling Bea how life had suddenly taken on a wonderful routine. "There is something pleasing about rising at six a.m., about having to steal private moments when Sunny sleeps. We're more aware of time. Isn't that right, June?"

Agreeing, June wrinkled that part of her forehead just above her eyebrows. She leaned my way and asked if I still wrote stories about my family. It was clear what she was driving at because Timothy is my only family, so I poured more wine and said, "Yes, profane and sacrilegious things: about our faith, our sins, the size of Timothy's auricles."

June giggled. "I love his ears. I love his little head." She pushed at Timothy's thigh with her foot.

Timothy said, his voice high and strained, "Thomas, for some reason, doesn't like me, or my ideas, or who I am. His way of saying this is through his stories."

The back of my head was sweaty. I looked over at Bea; she wasn't about to help me. She was staring at Timothy, whose neck was crimson. I said, "You're too literal. I'm the author, not the narrator."

Timothy shook his head. He didn't want to continue. He'd made his point. He said he was going to bed, and as he did so I thought of how everything for him was undebatable, which was why he had spent ten years in Irian Jaya winning souls for Jesus. I wondered if June was a Christian from the top of her rowed head to the tips of her long delectable toes. I wondered if Timothy was a missionary when they had sex, or if he went down on her, kissed her blue bum, and I thought, yes, probably. I looked over at June and she was finishing her wine, tipping her glass far back, and her nostrils were hollowed-out rain drops, magnified through the glass bottom. Later that night, as Bea and I writhed in the high altitude that made us want each other, I caught a flash of that microscopic vision and, in a sudden frenzy, licked Bea's nostrils clean.

The next morning we talked about butter, Noah and other things. Timothy wanted to make sure everybody knew where he stood, and pointed out that the flood had been universal, had happened in 3000 BC, that there had been only one ark which took one hundred and twenty years to build, had had three decks, carried seven hundred species of animals, and that was that. When he had finished we sat silently for a bit, and then Bea said, "I can't stand soft butter. You might as well pour oil over your bread. I like it after it's been out of the fridge for about ten minutes, and then I slide the knife edge-wise along the top so I get thick shavings that lie like pats on my bread."

June nodded. She was watching Timothy throw Sunny into the air. "Timothy won't buy butter," she said, "even though I love it. A tub of margarine is healthier, he claims."

"But you can't get the same shaving effect with margarine and there are so many additives, and it tastes terrible," Bea said.

Timothy caught Sunny in his hands, settled him to the rug and said, "And then there are the dangers of eggs and butter. About butter making your arteries plug up. Dairy products. Why do you think Asians don't have that problem? They don't eat butter."

I asked, "Was Noah Asian? He lived how long? Seven hundred years?" Timothy ignored me.

June said, "Sometimes I think I'd like a fur coat." She patted an imaginary collar and looked at Timothy. "Fox, mink, muskrat."

"Isn't she silly?" Timothy asked us. "She comes from a country whose average family income is six hundred dollars a year and she talks fur coats."

"Maybe that's why," Bea said.

"It's obscene," Timothy said.

I asked June, "Have you ever seen a fox, a beaver or muskrat?" She shook her head, and I told her she'd have to come visit us and I'd show her live ones. "Much more fun than fur coats," I said.

"In California she wants one, yet," Timothy harped. "In Jakarta I used to see rich women wearing fur coats. Imagine, forty Celcius. They'd ride around in their air-conditioned Mercedes Benzes. Huh?"

We sat down to eat toast and drink coffee. June sang a little song about a rainbow. Sunny clapped his hands. I thought about how everything for Timothy related back to Asia, to Indonesia, to Irian Jaya, to the little village where he used to be a god, and how he couldn't let it go, and how I was tired of him always using that as his point of reference; as if I and Bea, and North America, as if all those things were trivial.

After breakfast June and Timothy went for a walk and left Sunny with me. Bea read. Sunny was bright-eyed and happy. I put my nose to his face and discovered full and firm cheeks, giving off the scent of animal crackers. Blowing onto his forehead, I realized that contrary to what I had thought, decay did not begin at the moment of birth. The little boy I held was a well of life; his skin was tight from a healthy bursting of blubber. I burrowed my own long face (which was well into decline) into the child's neck, sniffing out the tiny folds. I changed his diaper. He flipped onto his stomach and I discovered the fur at the base of his spine. I cleaned dirt from under the fingernails of one of his hands while the other grabbed fistfuls of my hair. I bathed his slippery body, itemizing on the things Bea and I did and didn't have. I flicked my tongue at Sunny's head, at the part where the skull knits together, and I prayed for a baby just like him, same colour, same shape, same smell. All dressed and clean, he stared at me intently, as if to say, *Yes, Thomas, pray*, and then he shit his diaper.

I kept telling myself I loved Bea. Saturday night, the day after Christ's death, she squatted beside the fire, her hands huddling a brandy (June and Timothy had gone off to bed), and told me how earlier that evening Timothy had talked to her about children.

"He gloated," she said. "In fact, at one point I thought he was offering me his sperm. He doesn't seem happy. Sure, he and June look good together and touch each other a lot, but touching in front of others is a sure sign of trouble. What do you think of June?"

I lay on my back and considered a response, remembering her vaulted soles, realizing I was jealous of my brother; not wholeheartedly or even desperately, but I was finally admitting there was a corner of me that wished I could fit my palms around June's black waist and nose her flat tummy. "She's okay," I said. "I like her."

"Know what I find curious?"

"What?"

"That she's so tall. And beautiful. Her neck is so long. I mean, he's used to short people, and if he was looking for a replacement you'd think he'd have found someone a little more compact. She dwarfs him. Anyways, Timothy doesn't seem terribly happy."

I watched Bea talk. She was wearing a bright blue sweater, black culottes and red tights. I reached out and touched her leg. I said, "He's pining. It'll take him years to figure out life here. Maybe he never will. That's why he married June, because she reminds him of what he once was." I plucked again at Bea's tights. The light from the fire rounded her thighs, and I thought how lucky women were, to be able to wear pumps and panties and bras and lipstick and four earrings in one ear and short skirts and long flowing skirts. Skirts: the word conjured up for me a world of mystery and secrets. Men had such limited options. Black shoes, brown shoes; jeans, dress pants; tie, no tie. I envy all the things women can purchase simply for covering their bodies. I had taken to shopping for Bea because I appreciated more than she did the texture of cloth, the smell of cotton, the way a dress hung there waiting to be filled, the lacy edging on the underwear, the shiny newness, the hope for perfection. Bea wondered once if I should buy my own outfit, a little something to pull out for special occasions. She said this and then she laughed and called me a love. A *love*.

The final morning at Whistler Timothy said we should go hiking. Bea said she wasn't interested. She had a bad knee.

"Fine," said Timothy. "You could take care of Sunny and the three of us will go."

June offered to keep Bea company but Timothy insisted. "You'll come," he said, smiling at June and pressing her knee. She seemed to grimace; a white tooth peeked out and then disappeared.

"No problem," Bea said. "I'd love to spend the day with

Sunny. I want to walk down to the shops and look around, and then have tea and a biscuit."

So Timothy, June and I went hiking. We picked an easy route with a well-marked trail. Timothy was dressed in khaki pants and shirt and hiking boots. He carried a knobby staff; he reminded me of Rudi Matt – or Jesus. He set a quick pace and soon pulled ahead of June and me. June walked in front of me; she was wearing shorts, so I watched her narrow calves push out slightly with each step. Striped suspenders criss-crossed her back and, in front, pressed her chest. Sometimes she turned to say something and then I saw her face, bright-eyed and winded. She tilted her head jauntily and said, "Quite a pair you two, are you sure you're brothers?" I shrugged, breathing hard, thinking how high her cheekbones were.

She continued, "Timothy's so earnest . . . you're such an infidel."

I sat on a rock to rest and motioned her to sit. We drank from a water bottle and listened for Timothy. Nothing. I lay back against the rock, and some sun, falling between the trees, touched my forehead. I squinted at June's back. I reached up and pulled at her suspender, snapping it lightly. She didn't move. She said, "I love America. The shininess, the potential, the things. So many things." She paused and asked, "Did you know Timothy and I are not married?" Her teeth pinched her tongue. I was reminded of a lovely red lozenge pulled from cellophane and dropped into my mouth. I licked my lips. June had turned to face me, crossing her legs on the rocks. Her knees touched my thigh. I closed my eyes and concentrated on the sun.

I said, "I suspected that things were not as presented. Are they ever?"

My brother called to us then. His voice came from a distance. June stood on the rock and sighted him further up the mountain, directly above us where the trail doubled back. June waved and said to me, "I see him, he's waving like a madman."

I stood up, and June and I pushed ahead up the trail.

June's legs went back and forth, her shorts swished against her thighs, her elbows swung back at me so that if I had wanted to I could have reached out and touched them. But I didn't do that. I was afraid to.

Later that evening I was sitting opposite my brother. We were playing chess and I was losing, even though Timothy seemed uninvolved in the game. He kept looking at me oddly, as if I were a stranger. For some reason I was reminded of when we were young and Timothy had caught me lifting money from my mother's purse. He had closed the purse and pulled me outside into the rain. He had held me by the shoulders and called me stupid. Selfish. I had always been stupid and selfish, he said. I recall he was standing under the eaves and rain drops from a leak in the trough hit his head and rolled down his nose. A few drops fell perfectly behind his glasses. He never moved, never even seemed to notice, but with utter resolve hissed at me *stupid*.

Now, sitting there, I watched him. His expression was vague and lost, as if he had found a hard answer to an easy question. I thought, he is not a bad man, only a simpleton.

Finally I said, "Your move," and he reconnected. June and Bea were on chairs by the fire. They were talking about Guyana, about Jimmy Jones. June was polishing her nails, Bea had her feet up on a chair, Sunny was sleeping. Everything was quiet and peaceful and I myself felt calm and heavy from the day of hiking. My brother leaned forward and raised the queen, considering the board before him. But he didn't make his move; he only rolled the black piece back and forth between his palms. Then he stretched towards me into the empty space above the board and whispered, "June's leaving me. She told me when we were dressing for supper."

I looked at the chess piece now lying perfectly still in my brother's hands. And I remember thinking that I should say something, or get up and put my arm around Timothy, or call Bea and June to talk this over, the four of us. But I remember most acutely that I didn't do or say anything. I think I felt somehow that this had been my fault, that at some point I had made June see who my brother was. My mouth curled up in a half-smile of pity and satisfaction and I stared at my brother's small head. Then he shrugged, as if confirming that he was alone and that though Christ had risen for sure (as Timothy had told us earlier), his own brother would spare him no love.

We continued to play, the silence serious and cumbersome, interrupted only by the click of an occasional chess piece against the board. Bea and June had moved to the front porch. I could see Bea's arm through the doorway; their voices came to us dimly like a light through fog. I thought they might be speaking of June's decision. And then, pondering my next move, I wondered if my brother might have misunderstood June. I resented his exaggerating his own pain. He was pouncing all over my pieces in a frenzy, his thin mouth a tight white line stretching from ear to ear. As I watched his face I found myself hoping that he hadn't lied, that June was in fact going to leave him.

Later that evening after everyone had said good night, I lay in bed and waited for Bea. She came in from the adjoining bathroom and began to change for the night. Though I was pretending to read, I watched from overtop of my book. She stripped to her panties and stood briefly, turning the sleeves on her pyjama top. I admired her breasts, studied the bulge of her stomach, and smiled at her trenched brow as she worked at her top. I thought how I loved her at those moments when she was concentrating solely on herself; her face took on a studious schoolgirlish look: a sixteen-year-old about to apply herself to an exam.

She crawled into bed beside me and sighed back into her pillow. I turned the page of my book, tucked in my thumb and said, "In a world like ours, I wonder who is the more dangerous person, Timothy or myself?"

"Don't torture yourself, Thomas," Bea said, and she pushed her chin under my arm and closed her eyes. She was sleeping within the minute. No help from her. I turned off the light, stared at the ceiling and thought of how my brother frightened me. Sometimes I saw him as almost epic; bound by the earth yet always on the verge of breaking loose. I was not flattering him with this, it is just what I saw. He was also a simpleton, those striving to be gods often are; he was literal and dogmatic – my father had once said Timothy was a person in a dark room looking for a black cat that was already gone, only Timothy would swear he had found the cat.

I lay beside my wife and tried not to think of him. I put my hand on Bea's crotch and left it there. I lay back and remembered how, as a boy, after fighting with Timothy, I'd lie in my bed and I'd cry quietly to myself and wish terrible things on him. Often, what I wished for was that Timothy's big ears would grow even bigger, grow and grow until they'd become so heavy they'd break his neck.

Now, in the dark, I smiled at that. Then I leaned forward and began to whisper in Bea's sleeping ear. "Dream a dream," I said. "Dream that my brother's ears are growing and that with them he learns to fly. Dream that he takes off from this earthly vale and that he leaves us and ascends to heaven where he's always wanted to go. Dream that dream," I said.

COUSINS

SO, I TAKE OFF CONSTANCE'S SHOE AND SOCK, AND I put my face on her sole. And I remember my youth, summers with the cows, because her toes are sweet and warm like the milk flowing from her mother's hands every summer as I watch from the hay in the loft and drink in the farm. My Aunt Rose, a small, frail copper-haired woman who wears orange rubber boots and mucks out the barn, bends a creased and heavy face below the Holstein to suds the teats and fit the silver octopus, missing four arms, onto heavy bags. Abe, her husband, my uncle, wide-girthed and happy, chases calves into a pen, pailing oats, his black hair, wavy like my father's, falling over his eyes. And at the breakfast table he spills coffee in his excitement to eat and teases my little cousins with his imitation of a horse – lips flap, creating excited, angry children. "Stop it, Abe!" Aunt Rose's voice rises above the clamour. And Constance over there, like her father, ruddy and thick, she loves her father, she smiles. I am frightened by her smiles, by her interest in me.

Because my Uncle Abe was a tail-gunner during the Second World War and my father a conscientious objector in a logging camp, they refuse to talk to each other. So, every July, when the sun shines and cherries ripen and the valley is full, my parents send me. I have become a messenger, a buffer zone; blond and blue-eyed, an angel sent and returned. Another reason for rifts: one family prays (mine); the other, same blood, does not.

Then, at the age of twenty-two, after graduating from college, I work for four months on the farm. My uncle is sick, unable to perform the necessary tasks, and my cousin Constance writes me to ask if I would like to help out. Tired of hermeneutics and Paul Tillich, I gratefully accept and go to the Fraser Valley to find my uncle thin and gaunt, lying on the living-room couch, his hair greasy and grey, whispering to Rose who shoos happy children from the room. I write my father and describe his brother to him. My father sends a letter (Aunt Rose reads it to me), saying that God's grace knows no bounds and that he, John, is praying for his brother Abe. My aunt has angry tears in her eyes. She pushes the letter at me accusingly. I go out to mow the alfalfa, which is something I have never done before, so Constance rides behind me, a hand on my shoulder, talking in my ear about how her mother is tired and the plums are falling from the trees and rotting on the ground and three cows have milk fever. And all I can think of is my father's belief in the power of prayer and how even now my mother and he are probably praying in their house, empty of children, full of narrow visions, my mother knock-kneed on a hot-water bottle, my father opening his eyes later and bending to sight along the hardwood floor and, *ahh*, reaching out a hand to thumb the grooves left over the years by his own knees.

In our family, prayer can be broken down into two basic types, petition and thanks, the former getting seventy-five percent air time. My mother, who tends ordinarily to be more practical than my father, asks in her prayers for vague things like good weather, a movement to world democracy, and suggests that there be a massive conversion of the world's people to Christianity before the millennium. My father, who lives day-to-day in a cloud of dreams, is quite practical in prayer. He usually relives the day's events, local, national and world, and offers his solution, with of course the final option being God's. Certainly, there are answers to prayer. Even silence is an answer, and if the response is negative this is interpreted as God's will.

Constance's hand lies on my shoulder a lot that summer. It is a surprisingly soft hand, perhaps made so by the pulling of udders or the immersion in warm milk, and when, by the end of summer, her hand lies on more than just my shoulder I discover that all of her is soft and white. While her father lies dying on the sofa, Constance and I lie in the loft or down by the river, and she teaches me the sweetness of prayer because she does not pray aloud but worships things: the smell of cedar, of cow shit, the sweat on my upper lip (she licks it off), and freshly plucked peaches ferried into my mouth – "Here Danny, yumm, bite." She is red-topped like her mother, big-boned like her father used to be, and on those hot summer days we cavort, guilt-free, because we are young and invincible. We teach each other about love.

We milk at five-thirty in the morning. By nine we are hungry and trudge to the house for a breakfast of pancakes, bacon, toast and coffee. Aunt Rose looks beat. Occasionally Uncle Abe crawls to the table to sip orange juice and asks past grey lips how many cows are dying or if we're over or under quota, and then groans back to his bed. That summer Constance is flushed and happy, talkative in a dumb sort of way, which I don't really mind because I am infatuated; my eyes do not see beyond August when I will have to leave, go to a job I took back on the prairies. I do not see, either, that we have little in common other than the fact that we are cousins, and that we like lying together. Constance is nineteen, I am three years older, but we could be mere children the way we are behaving. It is as if in spite of the call of death hovering over the farm we will live life.

Constance believes that my father could heal her father.

"They have battled too long," she says. "My father has lost. And besides, wouldn't it be only right for two brothers to set things right before one dies?" I phone my father and tell him this. He sounds afraid.

And then one day he is there, my mother at his heels. He has thick, wavy black hair, a thin body, but his forehead protrudes like his brother's. My mother, stepping out from the shadows, greets my aunt and they hold each other and weep. Constance and I excuse ourselves and wander down to the orchard where the kids are playing. Constance suggests we pray. She is serious, so we do. Constance goes on about our fathers and how they must forgive each other and could God somehow maybe nudge them a little. I take a different tack. Uncomfortable with begging, I rub shoulders with the milky cowgirl beside me and tell God that Constance Reimer has pretty nice legs and if he would put his heavenly nose in that spot at the base of her neck and breathe deeply he'd die and go to heaven like I had so many times and that if he'd bite her ear he'd surely lust, and if not that he'd say she was sacrosanct or almost unpickable, and suddenly Constance elbows me to say that God doesn't listen to drivel, although she is smiling.

Supper is a solemn affair. Uncle Abe's hands shake as he picks at his food and tries to tell my father how he wants to buy fifty more milkers this fall and how I've been a big help this summer. My father, lips in his coffee, listens and nods, interjecting with polite questions here and there. Obviously, not much has been resolved. It stymies me, their refusal to forget the past: one man kills, another refuses. It was a barbaric time, a patriotic time, a time for principles. My father, of course, loves principles, which is why, the next day, when Constance and I are down by the river in a state of semi-dress and I look up from Constance's brown eyes and see my father standing, hands in pockets, up the path from us, watching us, I say, "Shit."

"What?" says Constance, looking where I look, and she sucks in her breath and falls slowly onto her back. My father doesn't move. Constance covers her freckled breasts with a crumpled top.

"Shit," I say again and bury my head in the grass and smell crunched clover and cow-dung and the leftovers of Constance, honeyed cream. When I look up again he is gone, as if he had never been there.

The inevitable conference is held and it is as if this crisis has suddenly bonded the brothers. They attack us. Uncle Abe has colour in his cheeks for the first time that summer. My father says, "This is absurd. Ridiculous."

My uncle says, "Things like this shouldn't happen."

At one point I say, "I love her." My father laughs, a big *Ha*, my uncle imitates him, and my mother looks shocked. Constance doesn't flinch. She looks out the window as if waiting for something. Aunt Rose is watching Uncle Abe with wonder. She smiles. Her husband is healing. He is on fire. His eyes burn and when he looks at me, it almost seems he is laughing beneath the anger, the disappointment, as if he is happy his daughter has been deflowered in this incestuous way; he is like an ailing king who has finally found a prince for his daughter and can now die in peace. But he will not die, he will live. It seems he is siding with my father in order to bridge a thirty-year rift. My father's hair falls over his eyes. He has important things to say. I sit and hold Constance's hand, looking at her white legs protruding from black shorts. She has a little birthmark, a mole, on the front of her right thigh. I stare at it. Find it comforting. I want to laugh, to stand up and say, "Hey, this was just for fun." But I feel a message coming from Constance's hand, one that says, *Don't leave me*, and I am hit for the first time by a sense of duty which is infinitely more powerful than love, and though I think I love Constance, I know suddenly I will defend us simply because that is what I must do.

All this time Constance is silent, her green eyes searching the world outside the picture window. Then she speaks, saying we will marry, and she says it slowly, so certainly, that everything is hushed and I sit there and hold her hand, dumbfounded, nodding my head, *Yes*.

My mother says we will have retarded children. Constance says, "Nonsense, look at royalty." Uncle Abe, excited by the idea of marriage, though doing his best not to show it, says that the wedding guest list, practically speaking, will certainly be small, mutual relatives and all.

My father is frustrated by this nit-nat and shakes his shaggy head. Shocked by the sight of his son and niece in each other's arms, he is now astounded by talk of marriage. His refusal to accept this is based not so much on the 'relations' but on the belief that Constance has no faith. "But," he blusters at one point, "Constance doesn't even know how to pray," and the group looks back at him with disbelief, and dismisses him; there are more serious things to be dealt with here than prayer.

But now the younger children are hungry and the discussion ends. While we eat supper, the weight of guilt hangs over the table. Constance picks at her food and excuses herself early. I follow, catch up to her as she walks down the road heading towards town. It is a cool evening and she hugs her arms across her chest. Her chin juts out. She looks young and determined. She is a simple girl, able to hold no more than one vision at a time. At this moment her vision is me, although if asked she would not admit it. Again, duty rises to my throat and I put an arm around her. She does not reject me. It begins to rain, a soft, slow, summer valley rain that makes Constance's hair turn brown. I think as we walk that I am too young to marry but that, nevertheless, I will. And there will come a time when we will share the same bed and have children who will probably be healthy. And on no particular night, after the kids are sleeping and Constance has gone to bed before me, I will walk into the bedroom and stand watching my sleeping cousin. I will think of how I had wanted to marry a French woman, an Asian, someone exotic who would have spoken to me with a foreign lover's tongue, had a different blood type, placed dark skin against my own white body and talked to me of God and books, not cows and children. Still, I will lie down beside Constance my wife and run my fingers along her spine and wonder whose prayer she is an answer to.

It is still raining the next day when my parents fly home. On the surface things look good. John and Abe shake hands, kiss. But the kiss looks like the one my father gives me when we are saying goodbye; it is Russian in origin, mouth on mouth, self-conscious and deceptively simple. I make a mental note to tell Constance that if we do marry she should prepare herself for his kisses. I leave the same day and at the train station in Mission I too kiss, but this is long and deep and slow and sad and hopeful and wet and forgiving and Constance is my partner. We tell each other very little. It seems understood that decisions have already been made. It is a matter now of Constance joining me when her father is well. I climb onto the train with my big brown bag and wave at Constance through the window. She is standing in the rain, getting wet once again, and as the train pulls out of the station she doesn't wave, merely nods her chin at me and smiles, hands poked into a slicker. She looks older, wiser than before, as if she suddenly knows her cousin is a fraud.

On the train I sit across from a young couple going to Toronto and beside me is a middle-aged woman going to Winnipeg. The woman is wearing heavy stockings and stout shoes with laces. She knits and begins to tell me that her husband died of cancer last month and she has just visited her daughter in Burnaby. The young couple is nuzzling and giggling, ignoring the strange pair across from them. I am suddenly ill at ease. The girl across from me is wearing a mini-skirt, and I can see flashes of panties. She is obviously braless and is wearing large hooped earrings. Her black hair spikes upwards and her green eyes flash around the coach. She exudes lightness, anonymity and quickness, feelings Constance could never show. Constance with her thick skirts and white blouses. She wears a bra, which I, of course, never complained about unlatching. Still, it is big and cumbersome, old-fashioned and heavy like the one this babushka beside me must wear. Now the old woman is smiling at me, winking about the two across from us, who stand and weave hip-to-hip towards the dining car. She shifts her weight and stale air flows from her skirts. She pulls out a knife, cuts some sausage and cheese pulled from a greasy plastic bag and offers me some. I accept, and as our hands cross they also touch and her fingers are soft and white, as if they lie in a thick layer of cream every night.

After eating I fall asleep and dream that I have written Constance a letter to explain that things cannot continue as they were in summer. I have plans to return to school and if we were to marry, I would feel trapped, as if she were using me to escape the farm, and that when all is said and done we are too different, she knows that, doesn't she? And would she forgive me my arrogance but we did have a good time, didn't we?

I wake up to the beginning of dawn, afraid, the clickety-clack in my ears. The woman beside me is sleeping, snoring in fact, but her head is lying against my shoulder, so that if I swivel my head my nose brushes her greying bun. Her hands clutch my elbow. I feel ambushed and try to shake her off, but she grunts in her sleep and hangs on tighter as if she is blood-of-my-blood or something. The young couple smiles at me as one. I want to damn their pity.

"Mother's sleeping, is she?" the girl asks. Her voice is softer than she looks. I think of excuses and denials: *Look, I don't know this woman. She comes from Winnipeg. She's Ukrainian. I'm not.* But I am silent, maybe because they look so temporary in the morning light, so modern and unencumbered, two strangers who will soon part. So I simply shrug, watch the morning sun, big and red, burn through the early haze and agree that, "Yes, Mother is sleeping."

LIGHT

CYNTHIA CUT HER HAIR THE DAY BEFORE SHE LEFT. Lot, her husband, came home from Safeway with two cartons of milk and some summer sausage, walked into the house and found her standing in the middle of the kitchen, scissors in hand, and one side of her head of hair lying like a black pool of blood on the floor at her feet. Cynthia didn't acknowledge Lot, she just kept cutting and carving. The bite of the scissors turned Lot's stomach. He walked past Cynthia, put the milk in the fridge, stared at the temperature dial that watched him like a blue eye from the inside wall beside the lettuce, closed the door, and leaned against the counter. Cynthia's hair, which used to reach her waist, was now above her neck. Lot judged it a poor cut. He moved his lips, *Chop, chop.*

"You have a problem with this?" Cynthia asked. She still didn't look up. She leaned forward and shook her head. Hair flew around the room and a dark storm happened. Lot didn't answer. He was looking at her nape, which was white and fair. It was a narrow neck, unmarked and beautiful in the way things can be when they are finally exposed after having been cloaked for a long time. He'd never seen her neck like that before. So he stared at it and thought, yes, we do have a problem here. Cynthia said she was going to shower. Lot swept the hair into a pile and filled two plastic bags. He balanced them on his index finger and wondered at the lightness of the hair. Or the heaviness. He couldn't decide which. He wondered if he should save it and, after some deliberation, stored the bags on top of the cabinet above the kitchen stove. Up there, he thought, the hair resembled a sleeping cat.

Cynthia came back downstairs. Her hair was wet; a few cuttings still lay on her bare arms and inside her ears. Together, she and Lot made a chef's salad. The eggs boiled and clanged in the pot. The knife clipped against the chopping block. Peppers squirted juice. Tomato seeds ran off the counter onto their bare feet. When Cynthia spoke she did so carefully, about nothing really, as if speaking to the hunk of cheddar cheese. Her voice was measured, like the sesame seeds in the teaspoon on the counter. Lot sniffed the air, sensing something, waiting for it. They ate quietly.

That evening they sat out on the front porch in the soft light of the coming dark and then went to bed. Cynthia, in a breezy, chatty mood, said they should have sex and so they did. Because of her new head, Lot felt he was with a strange woman. He butted her forehead with his chin and thought he smelled the steel of the scissors in her hair. Finished, Cynthia chatted a bit more, rolled away and fell asleep. Lot waited beside her. Waited, the taste of her still in his mouth. In the morning, when he woke, she was gone. Lot could feel it.

He walked down to the kitchen and put his hand against the half-empty cup of coffee on the table. She couldn't have been gone long, he thought, the coffee was still warm. For some reason this was reassuring.

That day Lot stayed at home waiting for Cynthia to call. He closed the shop, a used bookstore and card shop, feeling that his presence at home would draw Cynthia back. She didn't return. He ate Kraft Dinner and fed Toby the leftovers. Toby ignored the offering – he detested cheese – and jumped onto Lot's lap, kneading his thigh, drooling on his pants, rubbing noses with Lot, purring in his eye. Lot scratched behind Toby's ears and told him Cynthia was gone.

Eric, Lot's and Cynthia's fifteen-year-old son, came home from work; he had a summer job cutting grass. He sat on the bench beside Lot and asked for a beer.

"Half," Lot said. "And take your runners off, you'll drag grass all over the house." When Eric returned with a glass and a bottle of beer, Lot said, "Your mother's gone."

"Gone? Where?"

"I don't know. Silly, huh? I don't know. I guess she needed to go."

"You mean she ran."

"I guess."

Eric tried to comfort Lot. "She's been worried lately."

"Sure."

"Last week she told me everything was black."

"Really?" Lot tried to keep the pain out of his voice.

"Yeah," Eric said. "She said that and then laughed." He paused. "She'll come back. Probably went up to Brandon to see Aunt Susan."

"Probably."

The next afternoon Lot spent cleaning the house, combing Toby, watering plants. Cynthia's mother called once but Lot said Cynthia was out and promised to have her call back. Edith lived across town in a northern suburb; she was seventy, bull-headed and not often lonely. She came to Lot's and Cynthia's every Saturday noon for lunch. On the phone she sounded high-voiced and suspicious, but didn't question Lot.

Lot passed the evening on the front porch with Toby. He drank black coffee and smoked cigarettes, watching the smoke disappear into the light that was smooth as the coat of a cocker spaniel. He drank some beer on the porch and watched a thunderstorm approaching from the west. Inside he sifted through Cynthia's drawers, touched her bras, smelled her panties – even found a hair, a dusky thread, in one – counted the assorted bottles she kept on the dresser, and tried on some jewellery. She had taken little: her contact lens equipment, some lingerie, shorts, two skirts (the light blue one and the red mini), three tops (the sailor one, the sleeveless yellow one with the butterfly cut out of the back so her lower vertebrae show, and the black, long-sleeved cotton sweatshirt kind of thing). Lot knew all this, of course, because he did the washing, the ironing and the folding of laundry in the house. He knew what Cynthia wore outside and inside. He knew when she wasn't wearing something. She also took two pairs of shoes – her Nikes and a pair of sandals – a few pairs of socks, a plaid cotton jacket, her cosmetic bag with toothbrush, paste, floss and her medication, a towel and her VISA card. But she hadn't taken the Dodge. It needed repairs, and also Cynthia was too blind to drive. Perhaps she had taken the bus to wherever she went. Cynthia was fond of buses.

After Cynthia married Lot she tired quickly of being jokingly called Lot's wife. *Well hell*, she would reply, *that woman must have made a great salt lick.* Still, after the jesting, she felt some resentment that her husband wasn't a Roger or a Jim instead of a moralist running from Sodom and Gomorrah. But maybe that wasn't it at all, because Cynthia didn't put much stock in names. It had more to do with who she was, Cynthia, and how she was. Lately, she had begun to panic. She'd be splayed in the dentist's chair, say, the munch of a new filling being pushed into her head, and she'd think of the Seychelles or the possibilities of making love to a black man, and a frown would stitch her forehead and she'd become hot and edgy, studying the hairs in Dr. Martin's nose, thinking of Lot's nose, of how funny it was to be married to one man, all that permanence. But that wasn't really it, either. It was bigger. It had more to do with recognizing and not being frightened by her own image in a mirror. With travelling and not getting lost; with light.

Two years ago Cynthia started to wear glasses; black frames with thick lenses because her eyes had begun to fail her. The doctors claimed this was highly unusual but, of course, they found a name for what she had: an impossibly vague and un-pronounceable term that meant nothing to Cynthia. She went to see one doctor, a woman younger than herself, who breathed gently into Cynthia's ear and smelled of dying or-chids. She drew a heavy machine down over Cynthia's face and clicked the lenses in an efficient manner, whispering "good," "next," "and this," and bent to her desk to make notes. Cynthia pressed her head against the two black pillows cradling her crown and wondered how a woman this age could ever tell her, Cynthia, what was wrong with her eyes. She went home that day and told Lot she was afraid. "Jesus, Cynthia," Lot said, tugging at her thumbs.

She continued working, but in the evenings was listless and slept constantly. Lot found her behaviour disconcerting. He felt guilty; he had little patience for weakness and sick-ness in people he loved. Cynthia's problem was something he preferred to ignore. For Lot she was a burden. Caring for her was like repeatedly blowing up the same balloon for a child.

Cynthia sensed this. Knew it. It reminded her of when she had been pregnant with Eric and she and Lot had decided to marry. Oh, Lot had been good, fair and under-standing. Still, there had been this soft grumbling, a lifted questioning eye which spoke of duty, of responsibility, of entrapment, and she had felt guilty for carrying the baby, for not aborting, for embarrassing Lot in front of his family and friends. Eric, in the last while, was tending to fade away from Cynthia's illness. In that way he was like Lot. If you don't talk about something it'll go away. Cynthia saw the three of them sliding away from each other. And she didn't care. She thought she should but she thought too that Lot and Eric could look after each other. She had herself to consider. Just the other day she'd wanted to fuck her neighbour. Lawrence had been mowing the lawn and she sat on her porch imagining

him. She crossed her legs and pictured his shoulders, his calves, imagined his cock, thought about pressing its head
against her eyes, first left then right, as if that were some
cure. Then Lot joined her. He complained about the noise
from Lawrence's lawn mower. Drank a beer. Held Cynthia's
hand. Talked about Green Green Grass. Seemed terribly
happy. Terribly oblivious.

Eric, his son. His bone, blood, flesh. Cynthia's black eyes
repeated. Her jaw, long limbs, dark hair, brooding forgetful-
ness, easy smile. He had his father's hands; short, stubby
fingers. Lot's sense of inconsequence too. A hesitant, shy at-
titude that sometimes turned into meanness, into a dislike
for others. At times he couldn't understand why others
needed him. Friday night he was home early. Lot, surprised,
asked him why he wasn't out with Sonya.

"Because we're through."

"Is that good?"

"Whatever, I guess." And then he added, "Last night she
wanted too much."

Lot, a little lost, forgot to be cautious and asked, "You
mean commitment, or what?"

Eric shrugged and rubbed his narrow chin. "Last night
she took off her top, made me touch her breasts . . . and then
we broke up."

Lot wanted to laugh. He was both amazed and be-
wildered. He saw his son at the age of twenty preening in
front of a mirror, adjusting his own breasts, breathless for a
cruise with the boys. Lot wanted to shout that of course Eric
must fondle Sonya's breasts. My god, any boy of fifteen would
leap at the chance. "That's okay, son," he said, thinking immediately how stupid he sounded. He thought Cynthia would
appreciate Eric's story. She had no problem with that kind of
thing. There, see, even now he was thinking in terms of *that
kind of thing*. So, my son's gay, he said to himself finally.

He watched the news with Eric. He kept glancing over at
Eric's hands, his legs, the way his mouth moved. Normal, he

looked normal, Lot thought. He reached out and squeezed his son's neck. Then he punched him lightly on the shoulder.

"I've been thinking," Eric said, "that Mom probably went to B.C., to White Rock."

"She told you?" Lot asked, trying to keep his voice playful, wishing Eric would sit down and tell him what to do. Where had he been these past two days? Had they both been sleepwalking past each other?

"No," Eric said, "she didn't tell me. I just realized that's just where she'd go. To Aunt Elsie's house." And then, after a bit, Eric looked up and asked, "Why don't you go get her?"

Lot gave an embarrassed giggle and said that Cynthia had left because she needed to be alone, and he didn't think that meant her husband should chase her across the country. "Besides," he said, "she's tired of me."

"Oh shit, Dad," Eric said. "Stop pouting."

When Lot came downstairs in the morning Eric was eating a fried egg that was still runny. "Toby didn't come in this morning," Eric said. Lot went to the back door, opened it and made kissing noises. Just then Cynthia's mother phoned to see if lunch was still on.

"Sorry, Edith," Lot said. "Cynthia's left and all you'd get from me is celery sticks." He added, "Toby's lost too."

She asked, "How long has he been gone?"

"Out last night," Lot said. "He's usually calling at the door in the morning."

"I'll be right over," Edith said, and before Lot could protest she was a dial tone. He hung up and went to look for Toby. He stepped out into the alley and moved up towards Westminster, calling his cat at times, whistling a slow mournful tune in between, and at one point he recalled a verse, a ditty, about tolling the bell for poor dead Dicky. "Poor Dicky's dead!" was how it began. He circled the block and wondered whether Cynthia had left for good. He called Toby one last time and thought that he should have followed his son's advice and gone after Cynthia.

Edith was folded into the wicker chair on the front porch when Lot turned onto his sidewalk. He saw her grey head framed by the flowers in the planters. Lot stopped on the front lawn and adjusted the sprinkler, then walked over to the side of the house to turn on the tap.

"Hello to you too, Lot," she called.

"Oh," Lot said, dodging an arc of water, "Edith. Did you see Toby?"

Edith scrambled from her chair. She was waving a piece of paper in the air. "This came while you were out. Do you want to see this or not?" She raised her eyebrows and tucked in her lips in her exasperated way, as if things were simply too easy to figure out and why wasn't anyone else blessed with her clear-headedness? She met Lot at the steps. Pushed a yellowish paper at him. It said: *Catch me if you can . . . or want to.* That was it.

Lot read it twice, a third time, Edith's hot breath was on his shoulder, her eyes staring up at the three-day growth on his chin, and he wondered if his wife and mother-in-law were in cahoots. "So?" he said.

For an instant he believed that Edith was going to hit him. She squeezed his arm instead, viciously he thought, and said in a taut voice, "Where is it from, Lot? Don't you see? Don't you? Where?" Edith was wearing a light cotton dress. A kind of shift. It was a hot day and Lot could tell by the way her body moved under the dress and the way the wind shaped the dress to her body that Edith was naked under that thin shift. He smiled and wondered if she'd jumped straight out of bed. Her body was small and had certainly been touched by time, but Lot was surprised at how provoked he was. She was still bruising his elbow as he studied the paper. He saw *vanc.* and felt the claws of Edith, saw her shiny red, rarely driven VW Golf staring at him from across the street, saw her expectant eyes tracing his profile, and he knew then that her bags were packed and already in the Golf.

"Edith," he said, but her pincers got him again. She was pretty excited. So was he.

They left Winnipeg at four in the afternoon and stopped for supper near Brandon, then drove till three a.m. when Lot stopped the car and they slept with their seats leaning into their bags in the back. When Lot woke at six Edith was outside yawning and stretching. He joined her. The sun was already hot and high in the sky. In the distance a tractor and harrow slipped around the earth. It had been a long time since he'd been in the country. He thought he should have brought Eric out here more often. The space was frightening and sent a jolt through the body. His son would have liked growing up out here. The city was a claustrophobic mess that breeded shoplifting and homosexuality. They filled the tank and ate breakfast at a Fifth Wheel. Edith jabbered miles to the gallon and studied a road map. Lot watched the trucks and wondered why things happened to him the way they did. He thought how life's events fall like dominoes and a momentum builds until all sense of control is lost. He hadn't really wanted to chase over hill and dale with a seventy-year-old, leaving his son alone, to look for a wife who wanted solitude. Lot ordered more toast and concluded that Edith had made him go. Like Cynthia, she had some magical hold on him. Perhaps it was their hands, the length of their fingers, the pull of their tendons.

The following night they took a motel room on the edge of Calgary. Lot was tired and red-eyed from driving. They ate hot turkey sandwiches. Lot drank two glasses of milk and smoked cigarettes. Travelling that day, Edith had read, snoozed and talked about Cynthia. She had offered Lot harmless snippets from Cynthia's childhood. Like her penchant for yo-yos, her allergic reactions to bee stings, her need to sleep on her back, hands folded across her chest in case she should die during the night. "Ah," Lot had said, "but she still sleeps that way sometimes."

"Yes," Edith said. "She would." And then she became quiet and finally said she was terribly glad that she had had a girl. "I know I didn't want another child; at thirty-five, having

Cynthia was enough, and when I had her I thought life was perfect and just . . . just, yes, just. Oh, I know women get stomped on but they have their ways, better ways I think."

Lot had thought then – not really knowing why, perhaps it was this journey he was taking with his wife's mother and the fact that Cynthia was a hidden spot out there and he could think of Cynthia as a deceiver, as someone living in a lair luring him into her clutches – he thought then of Cynthia's light, which was so moon-like, powerful, old, moving things, moving him.

Lot lay awake that night listening to Edith sleep in the bed on the other side of the room, thinking that if he had been born thirty years earlier he could have married her and they could have had a daughter and maybe named her Cynthia, a beautiful, gangly girl, as Edith must have been, must have had a fiery, fine body when she was young, something to deal with, her mind too . . . and that's how the head works before moving into sleep, though Lot thought quite clearly that between Cynthia and him things had changed. That when they'd get together again, and he was sure they would, there'd always be this edge nearby they'd have to watch for. They wouldn't see it but they would feel it, like one feels an ice-cube on teeth even after it has melted.

The next two days they travelled through the Rockies. Edith had diarrhoea so they stopped frequently at rest stops where she spent hours in the bathrooms and Lot walked around knocking his knuckles on big cedars. He told Edith she should see a doctor in Kamloops but she said she'd wait till Abbotsford, no problem. They were going to Abbotsford not because Cynthia was there (like Eric, Edith was convinced Cynthia was at White Rock), but because Lot's brother Joseph lived there, had just settled there with his new American wife. Cynthia liked Joseph, and Lot thought she would communicate in some way with him.

They arrived on a Tuesday night; Lot had phoned the night before. Joseph and his wife Janice were watching TV and eating tortilla chips. Joseph sat back in a chair, smiled at Lot and worked a piece of chip out of his tooth. "So, you're Cynthia's mother," he said, looking at Edith. He asked Janice to get him a toothpick. When she got up and walked to the kitchen, Lot watched her move. He'd only met her once; the year before, after their marriage in Bellingham, Joseph and Janice had flown through Winnipeg on their way to Niagara Falls. She was chubbier now; she'd cut her hair shorter and was wearing less make-up.

When she returned she smiled at Lot, pulled her top down tight over her waist and announced she was pooching out. "See," she said, pointing, "I'm already bigger, ain't I, Joe?"

Joseph grabbed her and pulled her close. "And here I thought I'd never have kids," he said, and he looked at Lot as if they'd been in some kind of race and he'd just won, somehow forgetting that Lot had a fifteen-year-old son.

Lot shrugged and said, "Has Cynthia called or anything?"

"Yup," Janice said. "She was here for supper last week. Holidays, she said."

"Oh," Lot said. "I'm looking for her. She took off and Edith and I, well, we've crossed the Rockies to find her, hey," and he looked right at his brother and then at Janice, defying them to pity him, but Janice missed his look. She began to rattle off, using fingers as counters, what had been said that night and where Cynthia was headed. She looked so poised and in control, her little nose lifted into the air, that as a breeze came through the patio doors and pulled at her dress, Lot reached out a hand and touched her knee. Janice pulled back, looked down at her leg and stopped talking.

Then Joseph said, "Cynthia said she was going to White Rock. It didn't seem any big secret. She just said, 'I'll go up to White Rock for a bit and watch the ocean.' She didn't seem herself," he continued. "At least, not the Cynthia of three years ago. But maybe that's because I'm married now and all. That changes the dynamics." And he pulled Janice over to him and kissed her on the chin. She giggled.

Lot and Edith stayed the night and before going to bed they watched the evening news with Janice and Joseph. It was the summer after the Gulf War and there was a piece on the burning oil wells darkening the skies of Kuwait. After Joseph turned off the TV, Lot said, "Stupid," knowing he shouldn't but disliking the way Janice was prancing around all 'pooched out' and gloating, so he repeated, "Just stupid."

"Oh Lot," Edith said, "don't."

"Well, it is," Lot continued. "God knows the Americans needed a good war. Oh folks, every night I get down on my knees and thank the Lord I was born a wishy-washy ho-hum Canadian."

Joseph was standing in the doorway, a tea towel over his shoulder, licking his lips and watching Janice, who was punching cushions and straightening the living-room, preparing beds. She stood, her neck stretched. "It's funny," she said, "but I've always thought of Canada as something like a comic book. Light and unimportant. I'd say Canadians want to be like Americans, only they can't quite cut it."

Lot laughed. His face was red, his voice turned up a notch. "Oh," he said, "I don't dislike individual Americans. You know, Tom, Dick and Harry. It's the collective ego I can't stand."

"Enough, Lot," Joseph said. His pointed head was bent over his wife, who had tears in her eyes. Edith was glaring at Lot. Finally someone said, *Time for bed*, and they all jumped, not saying good night. Edith and Lot again found themselves in the same room and before they slept Edith called over in a soft voice and told Lot to go ahead and look for Cynthia on his own. She wasn't feeling well and would stay with Elsie in Vancouver. Lot grunted. At that moment he wasn't really interested in Cynthia. He was thinking of Janice and the way her neck was thin and long and straight, and how she'd looked earlier when he'd made her cry. He wanted to put his arms around her and press his nose against her eyes. And purr.

Cynthia began to realize that when she sold life insurance people rarely talked about death. It was all facts, figures, policies, interest, taxes, retirement. People didn't like to think about death. Cynthia remembered an older couple who'd bought from her. They seemed a lucky pair, as if loss were something they'd just recently discovered. In their apartment she sat across the coffee table from them, her folder on her lap, and was amazed at their kindness to each other, the woman's awareness of her husband's frailties, his soft dappled hand on her thigh like a feather laid on a dead branch, the shared shakiness in their fingers, the seeming weightlessness of their love, and their need to keep touching one another as if to hold each other down. Perhaps, Cynthia thought, age makes us airy, not only physically flimsy, but emotionally light too, the heart unburdened of the trifles of youth. Still, not once did they mention death.

During her time in Abbotsford, watching Joseph and Janice, Cynthia had been reminded of that old couple. Sitting in the apartment, observing Joseph stand behind Janice as he stroked her neck, Cynthia realized that we need another body to touch, to hold down, to help us carry our own weight, and she'd wanted to tell them, to say, *I'm going blind*, but the thought was pitiable, and Cynthia knew that after their initial "oh my's," Janice and Joseph couldn't help her anyway. In the end they had their hands full keeping each other from vanishing.

So Cynthia said goodbye to Joseph and Janice. She took a bus to Vancouver where she rented a room in a clean, small hotel downtown. She spent her days walking the beach at Stanley Park and her evenings exploring Gastown. She was lonely; she missed Lot. She phoned her aunt Elsie and was told she could use the house at White Rock; it was empty and the key was with a neighbour.

One night in a small seafood restaurant, she began talking with a man who was also a solitary diner. He joined her and they poked at lobster and crab. He was Quebecois, a visiting professor at Simon Fraser University. He spoke with a thick tongue and Cynthia kept thinking how Lot would not like this man. He wore cologne and gold chains. He quoted Rimbaud and Jacques Prévert. He said his specialty was Gottfried Wilhelm von Leibniz. His own name was Pierre. "Call me Roc," he said. Cynthia drank wine, listened to Roc speak and thought that this was why she had come here: to meet a man like Roc. He was Lot's opposite – dark, hairy, thick-tongued, crude. She aimed a wavering hand at the elusive flask of wine.

"Hold, hold," said Roc. "It's me," and he pounced on the wine, overfilling her glass, spilling onto the tablecloth and Cynthia's fingers. "Excusez," he said.

Later, on the street, Cynthia stumbled and fell against Roc's arm. He held her as they walked, humming a tune. Cynthia's stomach heaved. How trite, she thought, how comical. She burped and tasted cigarette and crab. She closed her eyes and followed Roc's lead. He asked, "You are sick?"

"No, really," said Cynthia, and she threw up onto the cobblestones, bending at the waist, resting her hands on her thighs; the image of herself in her own head was of a woman looking for something lost, a ring or a contact lens. Roc handed her a handkerchief. She shook her head but used it. At her hotel Roc held her hands and said good night. "Really?" said Cynthia's eyes, disappointed hollows in her pale, sick face.

"I'll return," Roc said. "Tomorrow even. Till tomorrow."

In her room, Cynthia sat on the toilet, head between her knees. Then, calmed, she showered, climbed into bed and thought of nothing more than the round purple circles that would be Roc's nipples, the strength of his Adam's apple, him breathing on her. She put a hand between her legs. He was nothing to her, and nothing was what she was looking for.

The next morning, a Saturday, Cynthia woke with a headache and a faint touch of the French language in her head. She ordered two poached eggs on toast and, after eating, suddenly felt guilty for enjoying herself. She walked to the local post office, scribbled a telegram to her husband, and then walked slowly back to her hotel. She considered that the telegram was a lie, sent out of duty, as old-fashioned as the medium itself, yet she also thought she wanted her husband to come for her, wanted him to chase her willy-nilly across the mountains. In her head she gave him a time limit. One more week and she'd leave for good, go to California or Mexico, take a job cleaning, waitressing, let her life go, sleep with the homeless, yes, that would be good in a warm place: sleep, eat and drink with the drifters.

Roc called her that evening and told her she was a good reason for Canada to stay together. He also said White Spot hamburgers were good. So they went. Later, in her hotel room, before they had sex, Cynthia thought of death and slipped a condom on him. It mattered little, Cynthia realized as Roc moved into her, that he was able to hold forth on von Leibniz, able to see hyperbolas and triangles that go A, B, C, to play with them in his head, to speak to her convincingly of the soul and passion, all the while stroking her knee with his own while holding the edges of her eyes with his thumbs, moving his hot breath down her neck. It mattered little. What mattered were the two bushes of hair over his nipples, his throaty laugh, a laugh that almost made her forget Lot, pushed out the tumbling thoughts of people she loved, arranged in neat parcels the confusions of soul and body. And, lying side by side after, Roc's hand on her thigh, she again thought of death, not of an instant orgasmic death but of a slow, tortuous, twisting fall into blackness where you dropped with no company, so that sight was unnecessary, useless, even. To stop herself from crying she pulled Roc on top of her, measured the heaviness of his hips with her own and said, smiling up at him, "Lick me all over, I'm made of salt."

This man she didn't know, this man she didn't really want to know, came to stay with her at White Rock. "I am coming," he said, "but it is necessary I go to Montreal in two days."

Cynthia waved her hand in dismissal. "Fine, two days, half an hour, one week, fine, good. Whatever." In the afternoons she would leave Roc, walk past the shops, over the tracks, clamber down the rocks to the beach, sit on a lawn chair, listen to the ocean and watch the sun. She marvelled at how the sun could not hurt her. Soon she would be able to do things her mother had always forbidden: stare into the sun, study a welding arc, watch a solar eclipse bare-eyed. There were some advantages to going blind. One afternoon she lay with her eyes closed and thought of Eric, how tender he could be, how Lot feared he might be too tender. Lot could be so squeamish.

Roc joined her then. He said he had made his bags. That today he would leave. Okay, Cynthia said. They sat for a bit and then Roc said, "Cynthia, you are beautiful." He took her hand. "But you are both light and dark. Halved. And me, someone, anyone, never knows which side he will face or enter. You understand?" Cynthia smiled. Once again Roc said he had to leave – and then he left. Cynthia listened to him breathing hard as he stood up. She didn't turn her head, just angled an ear and heard him climb the rocks, cross the street, start the car, drive to the airport, board his flight, take off. God, her ears were good.

Lot woke and stared up at the stippled ceiling of the apartment. Edith lay sleeping at his feet. The night before she had pressed a phone number and address into his hand and said, *Try this, she's probably there.* So he got up and dialled the number. There was no answer. It was seven a.m. Lot thought Edith might be wrong. Still, he let the phone ring for a long time and imagined that Cynthia was in fact there, lying and listening to his ring, perhaps knowing it was him, taunting him. He hung up, packed his things, left a note for Edith and another for Joseph and Janice. He apologized to Janice, said something about needing peace, and then he left. He filled the tank at the edge of the freeway, cleaned the windows of the Golf and chatted with the attendant locked into her glass cubicle. He said into the little silver microphone that he was going to meet his wife. She smiled and said she'd had a long night, a couple of crazies had vandalized a pump and kicked in the Coke machine. Did he want a car wash voucher? "No," Lot said, "I'm going to find my wife, and then we're driving back to Winnipeg non-stop, I have to feed my cat." The woman began to speak of her cats, three of them, but another customer turned up so Lot waved goodbye, tapped the tail-light on the Golf and climbed in. He felt lucky.

When he arrived at White Rock he headed straight for the house. It was a small yellow bungalow with a carport. The doors and windows were open. Lot walked up the sidewalk and peeked in the front door. He saw no one, so he called out Cynthia's name. Nothing. He walked in and over to the kitchen. Half a glass of milk sat on the counter and underneath it a note in Cynthia's handwriting: *I'm a mile up the road at the pier. Come.* Lot sat down by the glass of milk – it was still sweating and cool – and read the note again. He looked around the room as if to see if the note were for another person. A pair of Cynthia's shorts lay on the floor near the bedroom door. He checked the house and then went back to the car. He sat for a moment, thinking how Cynthia used to look with long hair, how big a chore it had been to wash and comb. He wondered if Toby had come home yet. He started the Golf and drove to the parking lot near the pier, feeling he was being pulled by a magnet and being wary of that tug.

Cynthia was sitting on a lawn chair facing the open sea. At first he thought she was a stranger, she looked so small, curled up, holding her knees to her chin. But then he saw her black head, the pale neck, the familiar top with the butterfly design on the back. The circling gulls were loud and even if he shouted she wouldn't have heard, so he slipped out of his shoes and socks, left them in a pile and walked to where she sat. He squatted beside her and she looked at him as if he'd always been with her, as if she'd never left. She told him about a dream she'd had, about people she knew who came to visit her who were naked and headless. Their bodies were beautiful, she said, only without the head there was nothing to give a sense of who they were. They gave their names, that was how she knew them. "I mean," she said, "how do you recognize someone by a toe, a knee, a breast? Finally you need some kind of light and that requires the face, the eyes, especially the eyes." She said all this as if reciting a poem from memory. She palmed her knees and pushed at the sand with her toes. Then she turned and said, "Come, let me look at you." And she took Lot's face in her hands and pulled him towards her, ate him up, working her way around his head, as if knowing that some day she might have to recite this too from memory.

That night they stayed at the yellow bungalow. They slept in a small bed and kept bumping into each other. Lot woke constantly, turning on the light to check if it were really Cynthia at his side. She looked like a young boy. Watching her, he knew he'd never loved her like he did right then.

The following morning he called Eric back in Winnipeg. "It's raining here," Eric said. "It's been raining since you left."

"How about Toby?" Lot asked.

"Yeah," Eric said. "Toby came back for a while, but then he left again." He asked, "How's Mom?"

Lot looked over at the sleeping Cynthia. "Fine, good," he said.

"Is she coming home?"

Cynthia stirred and opened her eyes. She looked at Lot. "Sure," Lot said, and he halted there, catching a flicker from Cynthia's face, a shadow crossing her brow like a sigh of resignation. She too had not slept well, aware of Lot studying her under the spot of the halogen lamp. She had thought of Roc, of Lot's disappointment when she would tell him about Roc. And she would tell him; in a mean way she wanted him to know. She watched him now, talking to their son, knowing they were discussing her, whether she would go back. Lot hung up the phone and reached out and laid a hand on

Cynthia's leg, just above the knee. He talked to her about their trip home. And as he spoke Cynthia felt the urge to move her leg, to pull away from his grasp, but she didn't, knowing that his hand was big, quick, that she could only slide as far as the wall and that maybe she didn't really mind that weight on her thigh, resting there like an anchor, keeping her from floating away.

LA RUE PREVETTE

TO GET TO THE BROOKMAN ON PREVETTE ROAD
where his daughter lives Henry has to cross a railroad track.
Today, as he approaches the crossing, the barricade falls, a
train passes, and from his seat in the Mustang he can see his
daughter's apartment block occasionally. He wonders if she
is awake, if Cliff is still living there. He thinks of his
grandson Anton, stuck with a male role model like Cliff.
Sometimes, when Henry gets upset, he pictures himself res-
cuing Anton from the irresponsible clutches of his own
daughter and her pathetic male companion. In fact, lately
Judith has been talking marriage, laughing lightly and flash-
ing this ring Cliff has managed to find, a tiny diamond that
sparkles like the front tooth in her mouth. She cracks her
lips, her tooth twinkles and she laughs, a careless, throaty
meow that reminds Henry of something other than his own
child, and he panics and wants to scoop up Anton and run.

Henry watches the railway cars, reads their logos.
Rosetown, Saskatchewan; Billings, Montana; Grand Prairie,
Alberta. These are places out there where real people live real

lives like he does here. It strikes him as absurd, somehow. He is fifty but still has difficulty thinking of the billions of mouths, ears and eyes out there that have nothing to do with him. It depresses him. And then, suddenly, without warning, the train is past and this too depresses him. "Whoever decided we can get by without the caboose?" he mutters. "Idiocy."

The apartment block smells of fish. Anton answers the door. He appears to be the only one up. "Where's Mummy?" Henry asks, folding the little body to his chest.

"Sleeping, Grandpa," says the hot voice on his cheek. Henry looks around, takes off his coat and finds room to sit on the couch. Overturned ashtrays and empty beer cans litter the floor. There must have been a party the night before.

A toilet flushes and Judith appears. "Is that you, Daddy? Oh Jes— I forgot." She bends to kiss him on the cheek. Her face is puffy and warm from too little sleep and too much beer. Her breath is stale. She is wearing a T-shirt and white bikini panties. Henry notices the panties because he can see her pubic hair sticking out. She has nice legs, his daughter does. She is barely twenty; still belongs at home, he thinks. Seeing her like this, half dressed, her physical self so obvious, makes Henry uneasy, as if this is not the child he raised so carefully, but a stranger who never had parents. Henry feels cheated. Judith senses his discomfort and folds her arms across her breasts.

Henry says, looking at his watch, "Thursday, eight o'clock, or . . . or was that evening?" His voice takes on a sarcastic tone.

"No, today, you're right. It got late last night and . . . " Judith spreads her arms at the apartment chaos, wrinkles her nose and dashes for the bedroom. Henry can hear her talking to someone. Male. Though he expected it, absolutely knew it, the knowledge that Cliff is there saddens him. He wishes he were a violent man.

He pulls at Anton's arm. "What say we go get a pancake? Perkin's? McDonald's?"

"McDonald's," comes the voice. Anton is a dusty boy; he always looks as if he has just crawled from a sandbox. He straddles Henry's knees. "Tell me the story about the cow," he says. But Henry doesn't want to tell stories. One ear listens to the voices carrying through the bedroom wall. There is a rasp of a match and then the sharp smell of a cigarette burning. Then Judith appears, fully dressed, brushing her hair, Cliff behind her, bareback with jeans. He has a wide chest and narrow waist. He grunts *hello* at Henry and snaps open a beer. Henry can't stand him. He finds bizarre solace in the fact that Cliff is just one in a string of many. Two months ago Henry had come to this same apartment and found a boy named Neville. Same thing: half-dressed, drinking beer, a sleepy, sex-sated glow around the mouth, a cocky roll to the head as if celebrating a kind of private coup. Hubris. The big fall. Out you go, Neville. Welcome, Cliff. His daughter is obviously hot or fickle or doesn't like to waste time – the pain Henry feels is tempered by the belief that Cliff will soon be history.

Henry pulls on Anton's jacket, his cotton mitts, picks up the car seat lying in the hall. "Come, Antony," he says, picking up the boy, "let's discover the world."

As Judith leans across and kisses Anton she brushes Henry's shadowed jowl. Henry feels spent, as if all his sap has dried up, he is a hollowed trunk. In his branches Anton is heavy and impossible.

"Five o'clock?" Judith asks. "Okay?" Her voice is penitent, she wants to be loved, she loves him. He knows that. He shrugs, steps out the door, his burden squirming, and walks away from his daughter without saying anything. He wants her to feel guilty.

She told him first. They went to a movie together and later, in a softly lighted evening cafe, cutting crêpes, she said she was pregnant. She was smoking as she spoke and he wanted to say, "Put that out," but instead he delicately snipped at a corner of a crêpe and lifted it to his mouth. Judith watched him, waiting.

"Well," Henry said, looking around for something to hang onto. He came back to Judith's mouth, her chin. Her eyes were black, confident. He sensed her relief at having thrown this onto him, knowing he would take it. "Have you told your mother?" he asked.

Judith laughed, a heavy cold rain coming down on a hard earth. "Mom? Really, Dad, you're so naïve."

And then, sitting there, being kind and asking the right things – he'd really rather have asked the true questions prying at his mind: Where did you have sex? How many boys have you done this with? Do all your friends do this? – they talked about the father, keeping the baby, and where she and the baby would live. The last one turned out to be moot because, just before Anton was born, Judith met a boy named Lee, whom she said she loved, and he, Lee, was going to take care of her. "Does he have a job?" Alice, her mother, asked.

"Sort of," Judith mumbled. "He's in a rock band."

When he heard this, Henry felt the usual useless flaps of anger and frustration, and then he sat down and pushed his thumbs into his eyes, and drummed at his gate with thick fingers.

On a Saturday in early April, Henry and Alice drive over to Costco. Alice wants to do a test run and then get her own card. Turning onto Ellice Avenue, Henry claims quite loudly that they don't need bulk food, or bulk anything for that matter. "What for?" he yelps. "Joseph is in Vancouver, Evan in Thunder Bay and Judith at the Brookman. Why do we need a fifty-pound bag of peanuts?"

"It's cheaper," Alice says, her mouth set on this particular vision.

Henry ponders this a bit and then says, "The place caters to people with money. You have to have a job to shop there. It's obviously elitist."

"Serving the middle class is elitist? Sorry, Henry, you're grasping."

"I've always hated this notion of being middle class."

"You need to be different, don't you? So you quit a good job and go on unemployment and drift." As Alice speaks they turn onto forty acres of parking lot. She thinks how her and Henry's life together is based on disagreement. He's always against everything: cross-border shopping, separatism, bulk shopping, church.

Inside they wheel a truck-sized cart up and down freeways. Henry manhandles a twelve-pack of tube socks and talks about dying before he'd use them all.

"Christmas gifts," Alice hushes. Henry mocks her usefulness. Later, paying for a bag of cashews and a twelve-tin box of tomato sauce, Henry announces, loud enough for the cashier and several other customers to hear, that the fourteen-inch Hitachi TV with the remote is quite a bit cheaper up the street at Majestic.

"Shut up, Henry," Alice hisses. "Shut up."

Judith phones one day to say that Cliff has won a trip to Paris and he's asked her to go along. "Do you think, Dad, that you could take Anton for a week? I asked Tammy 'cause she's often here anyway, but she's working and Anton just loves it at your place." Her voice has that soft but desperate quality that Henry knows can change to wheedling; it is the voice to which he will answer, *Yes.*

"Well, anyway," Henry tells Alice later, "I'm unemployed and Anton's great. Besides, I've always wanted to go to Paris."

"Oh, you've always wanted to go to Paris." Alice is ironing; she bangs away at Henry's shirts. "Maybe you should go back to work."

Henry smiles, feeding Alice's anger. "I like being at home. Sure, sometimes it's depressing, but the freedom's nice. In any case, what's the problem? You like selling houses."

Alice doesn't respond. She leans into the iron as if trying to burn a hole in Henry's shirt.

When Henry picks up Anton from the Brookman, Judith has left but her friend Tammy is watching Anton. Tammy is blonde, her hair is sprayed back. She wears pointed boots and torn blue jeans. Henry notices she has lots of earrings. Her face is thin, the look of possible neglect, but she still has a freshness and naïvety around the mouth and eyes, something his daughter has lost.

"Sit down, Mr. Reedy," Tammy says. Anton is watching "Sesame Street"; Henry calls *hello* but Anton is deaf. "A beer, coffee, tea?" Tammy asks. She is standing in the kitchen archway, her hands in her jean pockets.

"Sure, a coffee," Henry says. He waves his hand at the apartment. "Did you clean this?" Tammy nods and backs into the kitchen, poking her head around the wall to watch Henry. "I can actually see this wonderful shag carpet," Henry continues. "Did you know this was the thing twenty years ago? No, I guess you would have been too young. What? Two?"

"I'm twenty-three, Mr. Reedy." Her voice, Henry thinks, is warm and filled with desire.

"Such ugly stuff," Henry says. He feels a little strange to have this girl serve him coffee; kind of like adultery in your own daughter's place while your grandson watches Kermit the frog. Tammy swings around the archway and places a mug in Henry's hand.

"Hot," she says. Henry sees that her nail polish is magenta. He can see her white thigh showing through a large hole in her jeans.

"So, Judy and Cliff are in Paris. Wow." Tammy lights a cigarette. "They won it in a raffle, some kinda bingo thing. Cliff didn't want to go 'cause he doesn't know French. Judy convinced him. She sure likes him. Sometimes he's such a slimebucket. He's okay. You know him?"

Henry shrugs. He's still watching Tammy's mouth, which is working her coffee and cigarette. The TV clicks off and Anton appears at his side. "Grandpa." His breath is tinny and feverish.

Henry looks at Tammy. "Did Judith pack a bag for him? She said she would. Actually, she said she'd be here."

"Oh, the schedule changed. Left a day early. The bag's in the hall closet. Anton still needs a night diaper. Judith uses disposables. You want more coffee, Mr. Reedy? Come here, Anton, sweetheart."

"No, I'm fine," Henry says, watching Tammy hang her head over Anton's thin shoulders. Her eyes are open. They are a grey-blue, not hard, not too soft, like the sky's promise of a warm day just before the sun rises.

That same week the weather warms and Alice spends a lot of her time at the golf club. She is vice-president so the club requires her attention. She is a lover of golf. She says the game is full of hope, but Henry believes that more than that she loves the perfection of the surroundings: the greens, the nicely raked sand traps, the long fairways stretching ahead.

Henry imagines he loves Alice; maybe because he knows nothing else and their life is comfortable; they come together and fall apart and this, Henry thinks, is a sort of love. The week Anton lives with them Alice is rarely seen. Henry and Anton go to the zoo, the Children's Museum, the public library, the zoo again. They eat plain hamburgers at McDonald's, Kraft Dinner for supper, hot dogs. Henry feels he has never had such an unbalanced diet.

On Thursday they go to the airport. Henry likes the airport. He likes to watch the planes land and take off; it gives him satisfaction to know there are people going somewhere. There is no observation deck, so the two of them stand alongside the chainlink fence and watch the planes taxi in and out. The wind is brisk and Henry has to palm Anton's small ears. They talk about planes, about the pilots and where the people are going. They watch the luggage being loaded. Later, they drive out towards the cargo building from where they can watch the planes come in. Henry says how pretty a plane is, dropping out of the sky. Anton says,

Yes, pretty. A jumbo appears, screaming directly overhead, its wheels looking for the ground, and Henry wonders why a small city like his would have so much air traffic.

"Mummy went in a plane," Anton says.

"Just like that," Henry says, pointing. He wonders how he'd feel if Judith's plane crashed.

Later, sitting with Anton at the dining-room table for tuna sandwiches and rice pudding, he cajoles his grandchild. "Come, Antony, one more bite." The tuna hovers, Anton looks up, and the spoon descends like a swallow heading for its nest. Henry hears Alice in the foyer. She comes in and kisses Anton on the cheek. She brushes a hand across Henry's hair. This surprises Henry, who usually finds Alice distant. He wonders what she wants.

"How's my Anton? Where did you go today?"

"To the planes, Grandma."

"Really, love?"

"An' I saw Mummy's plane. Big. And, and, and . . . And, and it had wheels and a red tail."

"Wonderful, dear." Alice pours herself a coffee and sits across from Henry. She has showered at the club, Henry can smell this. Her eyes and cheeks look mischievous. She is going to tell Henry something and he wonders who's doing what to whom now. She looks good and in this he takes a crazy pride. Her mouth is big, like Judith's. She wears her hair really short so that the back of her neck shows, and her ears too. He watches her drink coffee and thinks that they haven't made love for a long time. This thought is interrupted as Anton clambers from his chair. After he is gone from the room, Alice leans forward and whispers, "I went downtown today, Henry, and guess who I saw?" She doesn't wait for a response. "Cliff," she sings, "and your daughter." She picks up her coffee cup with her long fingers and appears to toast the sighting.

"Ridiculous," Henry says, although as he says this he knows it's true. He detests the sway of Alice's shoulders. Her beautiful gloating chin. "That's nonsense, they're in Paris."

"I don't know my own daughter? And Cliff, well, anybody'd recognize that heap of cast-off clothing on the street. They were on the grounds at the university. Probably snorting LSD or whatever it is they do."

"Did they see you?" Henry asks. He is angry. Not so much with Judith but with Alice and Cliff. With himself. And Tammy.

"No. Fools," Alice says.

"You can't stand her, can you?" Henry asks. His hands shake and he wants to throw his coffee in Alice's face.

"Come on, Henry. This is your problem. For you she does no wrong. She's a tramp. Look at her. Five guys in the past year. She duped you into a week's childcare. She always dupes you. No, to be honest, there's not much to love there. Can't you see, Henry, she needs help? Not some kind of molly-coddling but real professional help."

Anton stands in the doorway. "Mummy home?" he asks. Henry stretches out an arm and pulls him in. Settles him on his lap. Tells him about cows and their four stomachs and cud and silos. All about cows. Anton likes that.

That evening Alice has a church meeting, and after she has come home and Anton is sleeping, Henry drives out to the Brookman. He buzzes the apartment and Tammy, sleepy-voiced and sullen, releases the front door lock. When he enters the apartment, Henry finds Tammy lying on the couch, watching a late night sit-com. She is drinking beer and eating chips. "Hi ya, Mr. Reedy. Need something for Anton?"

Henry sits down. He rests his chin on his palms and tries to look bemused. "Judith out?" he asks.

"Hey?" Tammy says. "Judy? Why, Mr. Reedy, you know – oh, I see. Jesus. You know, I told her she was stupid. I'm sorry, Mr. Reedy, she made me go along, she ... "

Henry closes his eyes and holds up his hands. "Don't worry, Tammy. It's not your fault. This is my problem. You have a beer?"

"Sure." Tammy slides around into the kitchen. She is quick and light.

Tonight, Henry sees, she is wearing a short skirt and a loose sweater. He takes the beer. "When are they coming back?" he asks.

"They went dancing," Tammy says. "Who knows?"

"Ah, Paris," Henry says. "Didn't you ever want to go there? Drink the wine, watch the lights? Alice and I were going to go and then Alice got pregnant with Judith so we said, *Wait.* We're still waiting."

"You could go now," Tammy says. Her eyes are sincere. She has sat down beside Henry. Their legs are touching.

Henry laughs, "Sure."

"You have a lovely chin, Mr. Reedy." Tammy reaches out a hand and touches his chin. Henry looks at her face and shudders. Her eyes are big and blue. "You have a chin like Judith's. Do you like my chin?" She takes his hand and puts it on her jaw. Her face in his hand feels like fine bone china. She is a baby, he thinks. He lifts his eyebrows and pulls away from Tammy. Stands and looks down at the top of her head. She has a habit, he's noticed before, of pushing back her hair behind her ears. It is a vulnerable movement, a nervous touch that makes her childlike. He aches as he watches her do that now. Her lips are shiny. Henry thinks maybe he should get down on his knees, and then the phone rings, a computer-like whirr from the bedroom. Tammy ignores the phone and pulls at Henry's fingers. Henry considers that it might be Alice, wondering where he is, but she's never worried about him before. He stands over Tammy while this ritual of pulling fingers and whirring phones revolves around him. The phone stops. "Touch me," Tammy says and, reaching up, draws his hand down on to her right breast, then her left. Henry is surprised at her fullness. He drops to his knees. He wants to say that this is silly, that she is only feeling sorry for him, but then she is kissing him and his mouth is like an open wound that needs healing. She smells like new earth. Her neck is hazy with down, her arms and elbows thin. He is puzzled by her giggles when she sees his grey hair; then she laughs, nimbly, carelessly. She moves him to the bedroom where they fall into the tangled blankets and Henry tries to ignore Judith's things: her red socks stranded on the carpet, her jeans flung over the dresser, her leather jacket at the edge of the bed. He finds himself hovering outside the movement of his own body. He notes the interest Tammy has in his feet, he compares her light hollowness to Alice's weight, he is amazed at her willingness – this is what strikes him – her willingness. Never has he met someone who has the same capacity to give that he has. He loves this best in the girl he holds. While having sex with her, he envies no one. It is only after, driving through the rain to his sleeping grandchild and wife, that he understands what he has done; he doesn't want to but he feels sad, and the sadness is like a keening that buries him and he almost drives off the Disraeli Bridge. But he doesn't.

In the morning he comes upon Alice at the kitchen sink. He pushes himself against her from behind, cupping her buttocks with his hands, and says he loves her. Alice is surprised but excited with his affection. She turns, puts her sudsy hands on his neck. "My, Henry, what is it?"

"We should go away," he says. "It's spring, we've got the time."

"And what about things?" Alice asks. "I just can't leave them."

Her sharp face baffles Henry. He looks for some turned-away edge to climb through, but finds nothing. He moves to the coffee maker. "Judith and Cliff never won a thing. Turns out Judith wanted a respite. You'd think she could have asked me up front." Henry's not really telling Alice this. He's thinking to himself. Alice is finishing the dishes, shaking her head.

After breakfast Henry takes Anton to the Brookman. A train stops them at the crossing and Anton pushes his face against the window. Henry wonders if Tammy will be there and is disappointed when Judith buzzes them up. Judith is silent, pulling off Anton's jacket and calling him love, squeezing him hard, tugging his ears, hugging Henry so hard he thinks of Tammy. "Sorry, Daddy, so sorry." Tammy has obviously said something to her although, it seems, not all. Henry feels now that he will always be hiding this from Judith. He sees it as partly her fault. He shrugs off her hug.

"I'm sorry, Daddy. It was an impulse. Really, Cliff suggested we do this, just to be alone, you know? You were free, anyway. Well, damn it, sorry. Okay?"

And that's all. Henry knows the pattern. Now Judith will toss the event from her mind and she will live as before, innocently. In that way she is like Alice.

"Mom told you?" Judith asks.

Henry rubs his temples. He is sitting on the couch where he touched Tammy last night and he keeps thinking of her smell, of how pathetic her giving was. Judith talks on: "I thought so. You know, we saw her at the university. She looked right at Cliff and me and then she walked away. We watched her perfect legs disappear around the corner." Judith offers Henry a quick, empty look and then proclaims, "I scare her." She seems taken by this discovery and pursues it. "All that ice is just show."

"Stop that, Judith." Henry, having deceived Alice last night, now feels a need to protect her. "She's my wife and your mother."

Judith presses on. "She's a golfer, not a mother. And a wife? Well, you tell me that, Daddy."

And then suddenly Anton is there, a bright coil bouncing on the couch. "To the zoo," he screams. "To the zoo."

Judith lights a cigarette. "Did you go to the zoo, sweetheart? Did Grandpa take you?" She watches him jump beside Henry and her eyes soften.

He dreams about her. She has the coquettish habit of playfully pouting and then moving him back onto the floor where she pops him on the chin with her teeth and he admires her dolloped whiteness. She speaks in a voice of pain and hunger. "Henry," she says, and then some choice vulgarities. He dreams of her asleep, her arm thrown up over her head, the blonde bristles of her armpit holding the afternoon sun passing through the window, and he whispers his love for her and wants to kill himself.

Finally, wanting to see her, he goes over to her apartment, several blocks from Judith's. She is out but the caretaker, a leer in his voice, says she'll be back within the hour. Henry walks down to Mac's where he reads *Time* magazine and drinks a coffee. He runs into Tammy on his way back. Her cheeks are red and her eyes look happy to see him. Henry feels the movement of desire on the back of his neck. Up in her apartment he rubs his chilly hands, then sits on them.

Tammy takes off her jacket, stands in the middle of the living-room and then walks over to Henry. She kisses him hard before she pulls away. She pushes a finger into Henry's chest and says, "Judith says it's pathetic."

Henry feels his bowels move. He wants to pee. "You told her?"

"She would've found out sooner or later. She asked."

"Asked?" Henry can't believe this.

"Sure, she talks about you a lot. She says I'm her surrogate. Really, you screwed her – or wish you could."

"That's sick."

"I know," Tammy says. "So what's your problem?" She is smiling, playing a game. She goes to the kitchen and sucks on an orange wedge. Henry thinks she looks like a catfish.

He sees things crumbling and begins to whine. "I wish you hadn't talked to Judith about us. It's private. Can't a man have one thing that's his own? A place to burrow into where nothing or no one will judge him?"

Tammy's eyes roll. "That's such crap," she says, walking over to Henry. She teases him, rubs her nose on his neck and murmurs, "She says you're afraid of death. That you'll die before her and that upsets you."

"Now, that's crap," Henry says. But Henry is drowning. He takes Tammy's neck and squeezes until tears push out, then pulls her head towards his and kisses her neck, touching the marks his fingers have left. Then he leaves.

That night he sits with Alice and watches TV. Alice makes popcorn and tells him about the deal she got on stockings at SuperValu. Together, they learn from the news that the hole in the ozone is growing and summer time in Canada is to be feared. Henry feels glad to be older; he figures thirty more years at most. He tells himself he will stop all recklessness. Tammy is out. Alice is sitting beside him, her hand on his knee. She is soft tonight, like the Play-Doh Anton had, soft and pink. She makes him coffee, rubs his neck. At one point she says, "What is it, Henry?" but Henry doesn't answer. He's thinking of his daughter and Tammy, shrugging their way through the night.

The next day at lunch, forking at her salad, Alice goes on and on. "Unfortunately, Henry, some children are bad. Maybe when she's thirty her estrogen level will drop and blood will once again flow to her brain, but for now she's lost. If you two didn't have this Electra thing." Alice holds up her hand and hooks it like an eagle's talons. "You've got your fingers dug into her skull and you won't let go. Shake her loose, Henry, or we'll all lose."

Henry puts his elbows on the table. He looks at Alice's mouth, the way it closes neatly over the fork tines, so deliberately delicate, and he admires her for it, for the control she brings to her life. To his. He goes out into a hot day and turns the soil in the little garden. His breath comes shorter and his chest tightens. The spade complains as he pushes down. Half an earthworm twists at his feet. He loses himself in his work, then stands and feels the sun. His knees ache. He has blisters from shovelling. The earth is hard and unforgiving. He goes inside and naps on the couch, dreaming of Judith's thighs. He wakes with an erection and the realization that people disappoint each other, that this is why we are on this earth.

He doesn't know who or where he is. He struggles out of sleep into the darkness of a room, touches his face, licks his lips in an effort to remember. Perhaps a smell, a taste will remind him. A body lies beside him. He touches it, finds it warm, a woman. He doesn't recognize the face. He climbs out of bed, thinks he sees a familiar foot. And then he turns on the light and it is the way the switch feels in his hand that tells him that the shape lying on the bed is Alice. The light confirms this and he realizes the phone is ringing and this is what pulled him from his sleep. While stumbling down the stairs he marvels at those few seconds when he was an unknown, a guest in his own body, stricken by the thought of being nameless.

It is Judith. Her voice comes in little gasps. She is crying. "What is it, love?" Henry asks. "Is it Anton? Is he ill?"

"Cliff," Judith chokes. "He's drunk and he was hitting . . . "

"Is he still there?" Henry asks. He is wide awake now.

"No," Judith says. Her voice is calmer but panic is still there. "He took my money. My wallet. He just left and I'm scared."

"I'm coming over," Henry says. "Listen, Judith, lock the door, put the chain on."

The drive through the empty streets is eerie. He thinks of Judith who, at twenty, has dug herself into a neat little pit. Funny how sometimes when he looks at her life he envies her. It's her passion. But not tonight. She has a swollen lip and a cut just below her left eye. Tomorrow the eye will be shut. Henry takes her head in his hands and holds it. He looks over at the couch and Anton is there curled up in a tight circle, whimpers coming out of his sleeping body.

"He woke up and saw the whole thing," Judith says. "I just now got him to sleep."

Henry brushes a finger above Judith's eye. "We should go to the hospital."

"It's all right, Anton's sleeping. I'm okay." She moves to the couch and sits down beside her son. She plays with his hair. "I'm sorry I called. I shouldn't have."

"Nonsense," Henry says. "What about Tammy? She could come over and watch Anton."

Judith's mouth lifts at the corner. Her nostrils round, whiten around the edges. "I don't think so. Tammy was with Cliff. That was the start of all this. I came home late and there they were. So I hit Cliff."

Henry's mouth is working past the heaviness of his tongue. He folds his hands as if begging for something and leans forward. "You mean to say Tammy and Cliff . . . ?" As Judith shrugs her shoulders and says something about this not being a great loss, Henry wants to laugh. He feels as he did earlier that evening when he awoke heavy with the fear of namelessness. At this moment he dislikes Judith a lot. She is ugly with her bruises and cuts, surrounded by filth. She deserves this.

"I give up," he says, his palms fanning the ceiling. "Look at yourself. Look at your son. What kind of life is this for a three-year-old? If you don't get out of this squalor, away from these people, then I'm taking Anton. Or I'll call the police. Family Services. This is stupid, Judith, and you've got to start admitting it. Alice is right, I've indulged you. You can't do it alone, can you?"

"Sort of like Tammy indulges you?" Judith asks. She has a careful, fixed smile on her face but her voice cracks.

Suddenly Henry feels too old for what he's doing, for the way his life has turned. Two weeks earlier he was a jobless professor, darning his socks, stirring up his lunches, sleeping beside a wife who was perhaps a little cold but a woman he loved, a woman who talked to him; he knew who she was. Now, he sits accepting ridicule and scorn because he has followed his daughter's lead. He studies the walls of the apartment. They should be patched and painted. He probes at a painful molar with his tongue and remembers how when Tammy's tongue ran over that same tooth it jumped but he hadn't minded. Excess has twisted his life. He doesn't recognize himself. He sees that is Judith's problem: she doesn't recognize her father. He sighs and attempts a last defence.

"And you, because of who you are, can sleep with anyone you like?"

"And Mom, what about Mom?" Judith is distraught. Surprisingly, Henry feels little pity for her.

He says, "You have no right." He feels his own terror, thinking of Cliff and Tammy. He stands and kisses Judith on the top of her head. He leans over and scoops Anton into his arms and carries him to the bedroom where he covers him with Judith's quilt. When he leaves, Judith is still sitting on the couch, tracing a pattern onto her thigh.

He sits in his car outside the Brookman on Prevette Road. He thinks how he has lived only half a century, how so many of those years were filled with hope. In a sense, it was the same hope his wife felt every time she swung a golf club. Now, that hope seems silly. He won't, can't have another life. Perhaps he doesn't even want one, not when he looks at the people around him. Of course, there is Anton. Thinking of the boy, Henry feels a fluttering in his chest. He takes the keys out of the ignition. He walks back into the apartment. Judith, a hint of query in her voice, buzzes him up. He enters the suite, goes to the bedroom, pulls the sleeping child to his chest, wraps him in a blanket and strides from the hallway to the front door.

"I'm taking him," he says.

Judith doesn't say anything. She looks both grateful and devastated, and Henry wants to hold her, to kiss her black eye, to scream. Sensing his weakness, she moves away and she says, her voice indifferent, "Fine, go, your lap was always deep."

Outside, the sky is breaking up into pieces of light. It is windy and the clouds are grey spectres skittering towards another city, another country. Anton wakes when the car starts but Henry pats him down. The Brookman behind them has the shape of a hunched-over, broken old man. Then it is gone and the city is all around them. At home, Alice is still sleeping. Henry puts Anton in the guest bed. When he bends to nuzzle the boy's soft, cool cheek, the part in the hair at the top of the child's head intrigues him. A heat emanates from that fine, marvellous natural line running through the sand. Anton shudders. Henry shakes off his shoes and crawls into the bed. He imagines he is young again and lying beside Judith after she has had a bad dream. He holds her hot body. There is nothing bad out there, he assures her; in the morning he will make her pancakes. Holding his daughter like this, Henry falls asleep.

THE COVER ARTIST

Steve Gouthro was born in Picton, Ontario, in 1951. He received his BFA from the University of Manitoba and his MFA from the University of Washington. His work has been shown in numerous solo and group exhibitions in Toronto, Winnipeg, Calgary and Seattle, and is included in collections of the Government of Manitoba, Manitoba Arts Council, Canada Council, Canada Post Corporation and the Winnipeg Art Gallery. His painting *Near the Forks* was chosen for the Manitoba stamp for the 1992 Canada Post Corporation's 125th birthday of Canada issue. Currently, Steve Gouthro teaches at the School of Art, University of Manitoba.

RECENT FICTION
FROM TURNSTONE PRESS

Some Great Thing, a novel by Lawrence Hill

Raised by the River, a novel by Jake MacDonald

Fox, a novel by Margaret Sweatman

Murder in Gutenthal, a novel by Armin Wiebe

Tell Tale Signs, fictions by Janice Williamson